Ann Cleeves

Ann Cleeves is the author behind ITV's VERA and BBC One's SHETLAND. She has written over twenty-five novels, and is the creator of detectives Vera Stanhope and Jimmy Perez – characters loved both on screen and in print. Her books have now sold over one million copies worldwide.

Ann worked as a probation officer, bird observatory cook and auxiliary coastguard before she started writing. She is a member of 'Murder Squad', working with other British northern writers to promote crime fiction. In 2006 Ann was awarded the Duncan Lawrie Dagger (CWA Gold Dagger) for Best Crime Novel, for *Raven Black*, the first book in her Shetland series. In 2012 she was inducted into the CWA Crime Thriller Awards Hall of Fame. Ann lives in North Tyneside.

Ann Cleeves

A PREY
TO MURDER

BELL◉

First published in 1989 by Century

This edition published 2014 by Bello
an imprint of Pan Macmillan, a division of Macmillan Publishers Limited
Pan Macmillan, 20 New Wharf Road, London N1 9RR
Basingstoke and Oxford
Associated companies throughout the world

www.panmacmillan.co.uk/bello

ISBN 978-1-4472-5313-6 EPUB
ISBN 978-1-4472-8908-1 POD

Copyright © Ann Cleeves, 1989

The right of Ann Cleeves to be identified as the
author of this work has been asserted in accordance
with the Copyright, Designs and Patents Act 1988.

A CIP catalogue record for this book is available from the British Library.

Visit **www.panmacmillan.com** to read more about all our books
and to buy them. You will also find features, author interviews and
news of any author events, and you can sign up for e-newsletters
so that you're always first to hear about our new releases.

For the wardens, volunteers and RSPB members
who help to protect wild birds of prey

Chapter One

The hotel seemed to be run exclusively by women but that was an illusion. The most practical and necessary work was done by a man but the women were so loud and busy that Richard Mead was never noticed.

There were three generations of women at Gorse Hill. Eleanor Masefield had been brought up there and lived there with her husband until he died. She was then in late middle age and he had left her with very little money. She could have sold the house, bought a convenient bungalow somewhere pleasant, and lived comfortably on the remainder of the profit. Instead she chose to stay at Gorse Hill and turn it into a hotel.

'It's my duty to stay,' she told her daughter, without explaining exactly what she meant.

It was not that she had a special affection for the house. She would have considered such feelings foolish. She felt that she contributed to the town simply by being there. If she were to move, Sarne would never be the same. Something valuable would have been lost. In fact she stayed through a kind of laziness. To move from Sarne would mean meeting new people, going to a different church, explaining who she was. Here her identity was already established.

Veronica, her only child, was the noisiest, most obtrusive woman in the house. She had none of her mother's calm and dignity. She chattered incessantly to the guests. They all knew her and Eleanor thought they tried to avoid her. The same stories were repeated year after year. Eleanor despised her daughter's weakness. She always seemed to be tired. She volunteered for too many committees –

the playgroup, the Sunday school, meals on wheels, all it seemed depended on her – but she did nothing well.

In her late thirties, Veronica had the sweet, enthusiastic face of a girl. Occasionally her absent-mindedness became so acute that Eleanor wondered if she were mentally ill. Eleanor had discussed the matter with Richard, Veronica's husband, but he had said that she made Veronica nervous and that if she were not so critical the problem would disappear. While Eleanor would have been pleased to believe she had such power over her daughter that idea seemed to her to be ridiculous.

Then there were the girls, Veronica's daughters. Helen was seventeen and Frances thirteen. Helen was shy, eager to please. Although she was immature for her age the adults left her to herself. She helped in the dining room in the evenings. Otherwise no one cared much where she was. Frances was dark, brooding and overweight. The family called her Fanny, which she hated. She knew her friends sniggered when they heard the name and when they used it at school it was like an obscenity. Her only passion was her hatred of her grandmother. Until they had moved into Gorse Hill five years before to help run the hotel she had been spoilt, doted on. Eleanor had pronounced her ill-disciplined and untidy. She had forced a regime of routine bed times, set meal times and limited television. Fanny had cried for the lost freedom, then become stubborn and wilful. To compensate for the grandmother's strictness her parents had spoilt her even more, helping her to defy Eleanor's rules, bringing her secret treats. Fanny learned to manipulate them all and in a sense her moods ruled the household.

So Gorse Hill had the air of an entirely feminine institution, like an old-fashioned girls' school or a nursing home, and Eleanor ruled it with a severe and charming authority.

Sarne had been George Palmer-Jones' home for the first eighteen years of his life. As a boy he had never mixed socially with the family at Gorse Hill, though he and Eleanor were almost contemporaries. He came from a respectable business family in the town – his father was a solicitor – and Gorse Hill with its parties and connections with the outside world seemed very grand and exotic. Nevertheless he and his wife Molly had been guests at the house before it became a hotel. George had known Eleanor's husband. They were both reputable ornithologists. George was an amateur whose first commitment was to his work as a Home Office civil servant. Stuart Masefield was a professional, an academic who in later life had given up his post with a research council to write books on raptors. George had never liked the man and had been embarrassed by the effusive greeting he received every time they met, the pressing invitations to stay at Gorse Hill. He had never considered Stuart Masefield a friend and all they had in common was the place of George's birth. Yet he had agreed in the end to spend a weekend with Stuart and Eleanor Masefield. It had been the spring before Stuart died. George had been editing a collection of papers and needed Masefield's expertise. It had been late April.

The weekend had begun pleasantly enough. There had been, George remembered, a good dinner followed by easy conversation about the history of that part of the Welsh marches. Even then Eleanor had been a good hostess. But the next day Masefield had taken George into the room he called his study. It was a square brown room with one small window which looked on to the hillside. It had the same smell and the same jumble of exhibits as a poor provincial museum. It shocked George profoundly. Two shotguns stood in one corner. On wooden shelves there were rows of stuffed birds of prey, with several examples of the same species, especially golden eagle, buzzard and peregrine. On the walls were a series of photographs of birds on the nest and in two large cabinets tray after tray of raptors' eggs, many arranged in complete clutches, all carefully labelled. It seemed to George then that the man's interest in birds was acquisitive, possessive.

'Aren't these illegal?' George had asked.

Masefield smiled secretively, became for George a cartoon of a miser. 'Oh no,' he said smoothly. 'None of them were taken illegally, you know. And they're all essential for my research.'

Immediately afterwards Masefield had insisted on taking George for a walk. George had not wanted to go but almost rudely Masefield refused to listen to his excuses. They had walked together through a blustery west wind up the hill behind the house. There was a steep, rocky outcrop, a cliff face in the hillside, and halfway up the bare rock was a peregrine eyrie. Peregrines were rarer then, still suffering from the widespread use of pesticides, and on an inland English site in the south were unknown. Despite his distaste for Masefield, George was thrilled to watch the male peregrine carry a pigeon to its plucking post, then fly off again towards Wales.

'They came back last year,' Masefield shouted above the wind. 'There was an eyrie here in Elizabethan times. I knew they would come back.'

His voice was altered, uncontrolled. It was as if the birds had belonged to him, as if in some way he had drawn them back to him. George felt the man was unbalanced and felt suddenly sorry for Eleanor. He suffered the rest of the weekend with unease and did not return to Gorse Hill until after Masefield's death.

They returned quite regularly when the place was a hotel. George had an elderly aunt in a nursing home in Sarne and they visited her for ritual conversation and afternoon tea. No other relatives were left in the town, so Gorse Hill was the natural place to stay. Besides, George thought they should support Eleanor. He admired her cool efficiency and independence. He was attracted to her elegance. He thought he had been attracted to her since their first meeting. He never discussed Eleanor with his wife but Molly seemed to accept that he enjoyed Eleanor's company and never objected to staying at the hotel. The food was excellent and she seemed not to mind listening to Veronica's stories. During their marriage she had never expressed jealousy. She must have known that in fact there was no competition. It seemed to their acquaintances in Sarne that Eleanor was a friend of them both.

Nevertheless, they were surprized when Eleanor summoned them to Gorse Hill. It was spring, almost exactly the same time of year as their first visit. George recognized her voice at once – imperious, attractive and a little older.

'George,' she said, as soon as he picked up the phone and gave his name. 'You and Molly must come to Gorse Hill again. As my guests.'

'That's very kind,' he said politely. 'Perhaps in the autumn . . .'

'You don't understand,' she said. 'I'm concerned about the peregrines, Stuart's peregrines. The eggs hatched yesterday. I think someone intends to take the young.'

'Have you been in touch with the RSPB?'

'Of course.' She was utterly dismissive. 'Some impertinent young man told me that there are so many peregrines breeding in Britain now that it's impossible to warden every vulnerable site.'

It was true. The decline in the use of some pesticides meant that the peregrine was no longer such a rare bird.

'I suppose,' George said, 'that the society only has limited resources.'

'I want to hire you, George,' she said. She shouted so that she seemed older than she was, as if she came from a generation unused to the telephone. 'You're a private detective. Come and look after the birds for me. I don't want anything to happen to Stuart's birds.'

George disliked the term 'private detective' and never used it. After retiring from his post in the Home Office, when he had worked closely with the police, he had thought there would be excitement enough in bird-watching, in finding rare birds, but he had missed the challenge of work. Now he and Molly ran an advice agency which had come to specialize in missing teenagers. George still had contacts in the legal profession who referred clients to him. He never had to advertise for work but the agency was never so busy that he felt he could turn business away. He hesitated.

'I don't know what we could do,' he said.

'Please, George,' she said, as appealing suddenly as a young girl. 'Please come. I need your help.'

There was an edge of desperation in her voice which made him think that the peregrines were only an excuse and that she may be in some real trouble. Perhaps it was in an attempt to appear gallant, to match the old-fashioned helplessness of her summons, that he said immediately: 'Of course. Of course we'll come.' Perhaps he only needed an excuse to enjoy her company.

Across the table in their untidy kitchen where most of the agency's work was done, Molly looked at him and smiled at his weakness.

As they drove down the hill into Sarne it seemed to George that it had scarcely changed since his childhood. They arrived in the early evening and the town was empty. It had been a sunny day in mid May, but now the sun was filtered through a grey haze of thin cloud. The town was surrounded by hills and to the west, beyond Gorse Hill the hills became higher where Powys began. It seemed to George that the town was always in shadow. That was how he remembered it, a series of grey houses and small, shuttered shops, where he would be taken by his aunts who would purchase small items and exchange patronizing pleasantries with the shopkeepers. His mother had died when he was a child and he had been brought up by his father and his spinster aunts. Now everything seemed smaller and rather shabby. The high street was narrow and no major chain stores had been attracted there. One of the shops was boarded up. Perhaps the new by-pass had been bad for business. The cattle market which had seemed an immense and exciting place in childhood was passed in a flash without notice. Of course he had been back to Sarne many times since he had left it, with great relief at eighteen, but each time he returned it seemed to have shrunk and grown more dingy.

Molly was driving. She manoeuvred past the parked cars in the high street, then the road climbed steeply again past the church. He had enjoyed going to church. It had at least given a taste of something more than small business and gossip. He must have seen Eleanor's parents there, perhaps Eleanor herself because she still attended, but he could drag no image of them from his memory.

Past the church the road forked. One way joined the by-pass and continued to Radnor. The other climbed again to Gorse Hill. It was unfenced and led up through banks of gorse and the twisted stems of trees misshaped by the wind. It ended in a barn and a footpath. Just before the barn was the entrance to Gorse Hill. The house was hidden from the road by a fold in the land and a garden full of trees. It was like an oasis in the bleak, uncultivated sweep of the hill.

Two stone pillars marked the entrance to the hotel. They were worn by age and the wind and covered in moss and lichen. They seemed much older than the house itself. Carved at the top of one of the pillars was the head of a falcon. George had seen it before but that evening it had a special significance. In the strange light it was possible to believe that there was some magical, mysterious connection between the falcons and the man who had owned the land where they bred.

Without comment Molly drove between the pillars and turned the bend in the drive so that they could see the house and the high wall of the hill behind. The house was large, Victorian and rather ugly. It was the setting which made it imposing. At one end there was a large glass conservatory which reflected the misty evening sunlight. The house was beautifully maintained. George saw that it had been freshly painted since they had last visited and the gardens were immaculate. An expensive new car was parked in the Masefields' private garage at the back of the house.

So Eleanor is making a go of it, he thought, with an almost personal pride in the woman's achievement. I always knew she would.

As the car pulled up Veronica rushed out of the double front door to greet them. She appeared so quickly that she must have been watching for them from the kitchen window. She was wearing a flowered overall. She must have been preparing flowers for the dinner table because as she ran down the steps on to the gravel she was carrying a pair of scissors in one hand.

'I'm so glad you've come,' Veronica said in a breathless stage whisper, her pretty anxious face pushed through the window so that it was close to George's. 'Mother's been behaving very oddly. I think she might be mad.'

Helen was in her room, preparing for work, thinking of Laurie. I should write this down, she thought, I should write down how I feel today because nothing so wonderful will ever happen to me again. Old people never feel like this. When I'm older I want to remember what it was like. But she did not write. She remembered the day again, hesitating in her mind to find the words to describe it, so that when she did record what had happened she would get it right.

Laurie had asked her to show him the peregrines. She must have told him about them in one of their long conversations. He had waited until they were alone to ask her, but the invitation, if it was an invitation, was casually given.

'I was thinking of going for a walk on the hill tomorrow,' he had said, whispering across the table to her in the school library. 'Why don't you come too? You could show me your peregrines. I'd like you to come.'

Laurie was in a different crowd from her at school. She worked hard. She would go to university, perhaps even to Oxford. He was in the sixth form to re-sit O levels. His only A level subject was music. He was brilliant at music. Everyone knew that.

Her grandmother had wanted to send Helen to the private school where Veronica had been educated as a boarder, but for once her parents had stood up to Eleanor. The girls could decide, they said. And the girls had chosen the comprehensive in Sarne, probably because that was what Eleanor had least wanted. Helen had never had a real boyfriend. She had been out with other boys at school, but no one she was serious about, no one who cared about her. Laurie was different.

It was a hot shimmering day, the first very hot day of the spring. The Welsh mountains were hidden by a heat haze by mid morning. She had not known how to dress. She was always aware that she had none of the flair or style of her friends and that in comparison with them she looked staid and uninteresting. In the end she had decided on the clothes she would have worn for a walk on her own – jeans and a T-shirt and sandals. She went to the kitchen to pack a picnic. She had agonized too over that. Perhaps Laurie had only planned to spend an hour with her and to come prepared for a day would seem a foolish presumption. But he need never know. If he left her before lunch time, the picnic could stay in the rucksack.

Laurie's mother was in the kitchen, supervising the serving of breakfast. Mrs Oliver had worked at Gorse Hill since the hotel had opened and her mother had worked there before, for Eleanor's parents. Helen had always been intimidated by the woman. She was stern and humourless and – helped by a couple of teenagers from Sarne – it seemed to Helen that she did most of the work in the kitchen. Eleanor and Veronica planned the menus and added elegant finishing touches but it was Nan Oliver, her face red from the heat, who chopped and kneaded and stirred according to their instructions. Helen wondered if Laurie had told his mother that they were meeting. If he had, Mrs Oliver made no comment, and only watched as Helen packed cold meat and salad into containers, helped herself to cakes from the tin in the larder.

On her way out of the house she met her father who was coming out of the office. He was a tall man, with a long face, like a horse's, and thinning sandy hair. It seemed to Helen that he looked strained and tired. It was a busy time of the year, the start of the season, and he did all the bookings and accounts, all the buying.

'You don't look very well,' she said. He was so quiet and dependable that they took him for granted.

'Oh,' he said. 'I'm fine.' He looked at her rucksack, at the thin jacket she carried over her shoulders.

'Will you be out all day?' he asked. 'You know it's the Wildlife Trust Open Day tomorrow. Your grandmother will expect you to be here to help.'

'I don't know,' she said. 'I'm going for a walk on the hill.'

'On your own?'

'No,' she said and could feel herself blushing. 'With a friend.'

'Enjoy yourself,' he said. 'Really. Have a lovely day.' He smiled at her. 'Stay out as long as you like. Eleanor will have to manage without you.'

She had arranged to meet Laurie by the barn where the footpath started. The grass around the building was long and mixed with clover and buttercups. Before they had moved to Gorse Hill her father had run his own photographic business in Sarne and they had come to Gorse Hill every Sunday for lunch. She remembered picking huge bunches of clover and buttercups to take home to the town with her and being disappointed because they died in the car. She reached the footpath before Laurie, and sat on the grass where they had arranged to meet and waited for him. Everywhere there was a sickly scent of gorse.

Perhaps she had fallen asleep for a moment or perhaps she was just dazed by the unaccustomed heat and the sunshine, because she did not hear him approach. She felt his hand on her shoulder and turned to face him, so shocked that she had no time to prepare the way she looked or to say the things she had planned. He had never touched her before. They had talked for hours but they had never touched. He stood above her, blocking out the sun. He was wearing jeans and a black T-shirt with a Greenpeace slogan on the front. In those few moments she thought she saw everything about him in sharp detail. Perhaps even then she knew that she would want to remember it all clearly and write it all down. She stood up.

'I wasn't sure you'd come,' he said. It occurred to her for the first time that he might be as nervous as she was.

'You should have known that I would,' Helen said.

He took her hand and they walked together up the footpath. It was well worn, used by ramblers looking for Offa's Dyke, eroded in places to the bare rock. He knew more about birds than she did and pointed out meadow pipit, skylark, lapwing. Away from the field around the barn which had once been cultivated, there was only bracken, rough grassland and a few sheep. The path was very steep and soon they were high above Gorse Hill looking down on the roof of the house. She was lightheaded with the effort of climbing and the heady scent of the gorse.

'Does your grandmother own this land?' he asked.

'Yes,' she said. 'All the way to the top of the hill. But she lets the grazing to a farmer.'

'Well,' he said gently. 'Where's your peregrine eyrie?'

The footpath flattened, crossed the face of the hill before reaching the summit and led into the next valley, but above them the hill became more sheer and rocky. It might perhaps have been possible to climb there without a rope. There were buttresses and shady slopes and crevices where there were still grass and birch saplings, but from where they were standing that seemed impossible. Halfway up the cliff, in a narrow fold in the rock, was the eyrie. With the naked eye they could only see the white stain of dropping and an indistinct grey shape which might have been the female, but Laurie seemed not to mind.

'It's terrific,' he said. 'What a beautiful view she must have right over the valley. Next time we come we'll try to get some binoculars.'

'My grandmother has some,' she said. 'I'll borrow hers.' She did not want to appear too excited about his plans for future visits to the eyrie. Perhaps he was only interested in the falcons and she was deluding herself that he liked her.

They found a place to sit just below the path, behind a big, pink smooth boulder. They were hidden from the path there and looked down over Gorse Hill and the town. It was, Helen thought, their own eyrie. He put his arm around her bare shoulders and kissed her. His lips and his face were warm.

They spent most of the day there. They shared the picnic and talked and kissed and lay on their stomachs to look at the view. A group of racing pigeons flew over and the small male peregrine appeared from nowhere, separated one brilliant white pigeon from the crowd and killed it from below. It was over so quickly that she might not have noticed what was happening if Laurie had not pointed it out to her.

'How do you know so much about birds?' she asked.

'My dad was keen,' he said. 'He used to take us out when we were kids.'

'You won't tell anyone about the nest, will you?' she said suddenly. 'My grandmother's afraid someone's going to steal the young.'

'Of course not,' he said. 'Who would want to steal them?'

'I don't know,' she said vaguely. 'Falconers I suppose.'

'Why does your grandmother think they're in danger?'

'She said there was a van she didn't recognize parked at the end of the lane near the barn on two evenings last week. It was an old blue van with a registration number from outside the area.'

'Did she contact the police?'

'I don't know. She might have done. She seems suddenly to be obsessed by the birds. She never bothered much when Grandpa was alive and he was the one with the real interest. Now she's trying to persuade us all to take turns at guarding the eyrie. My parents think she's going loopy.'

'Do you?'

'I don't know. Something's happening. She's usually so cool and proper. She's been secretary of the Sarne Wildlife Trust for ages but I thought she enjoyed the social events and that she wasn't really committed. The Trust is holding its Open Day at Gorse Hill tomorrow. She's making herself very unpopular with the other members because she's trying to persuade them that all the money they raise at the Open Day should go to pay a warden to protect the peregrines.'

'I'm coming tomorrow,' he said quietly. 'To the Open Day. The Trust has asked the Folk Club to do some music. I'll be singing. You don't mind?'

'No,' she cried. 'Of course I don't mind.'

'I was afraid,' he said, 'that your parents might not like me.'

'Of course they'll like you,' she said, then added: 'Besides, it's not them that matter. It's Grandmother.'

She returned to the hotel to find it transformed. A marquee had been erected on the lawn and a man with patched jeans was testing a public-address system. Fanny was in disgrace because she had eaten six meringues which had been prepared for the following day. Eleanor was directing operations and the committee of the Wildlife Trust were gathered around her. None of that mattered. Helen sat by the open window, listening to the unfamiliar shouting and noise in the garden below, then dressed for work in the dining room. All the time she dreamt of Laurie.

Laurie walked home. His pleasure in the day was spoilt by an unease, a peculiar sense of threat, because an old blue van had been seen near Gorse Hill. His father had driven an old blue van and he had hoped never to see his father again. It was not even that he thought his father was in Sarne. It was that the memory of the van had brought back memories of his father and they made him feel angry and depressed. His father always lingered at the back of his mind as an unresolved and troublesome problem. He tried to bury the memories again and to think instead of Helen.

He had not let himself believe that Helen would meet him. What could she have in common with him? Her parents were rich, she spoke well, passed every exam she sat. He had not come across her in school until they were both in the sixth form. He had spent most of his childhood in Wolverhampton and by the time he arrived at the high school most of the friendships were already established. He mixed in a different group. She seemed aloof. He had heard of her of course from his mother, but he suspected she would look down on him. They had first become friends the Christmas before during the rehearsals for the school play. It was *The Good Woman of Setzuan* by Brecht. He was arranging the music. Helen had a small acting part. They sat in a corner of the hall while the others rehearsed and they talked – first about the play and his music and then about other things. He could not think of her without remembering the smell of the varnish on the floor of the hall and of the rubber gym mats piled in the corners where they sat.

He had come to like her very much. She represented everything he had ever wanted – strength, a real family. He thought about her all the time until he was nearly ill and his mother asked him sharply what was the matter with him. In the end he knew he would have to ask Helen to go out with him even if she turned him down. So the day had been special, unbelievable, until the mention of the old blue van had reminded him of the differences between them.

He lived on a small council estate on the low damp ground near the river. In the winter the river flooded the opposite bank so that the line of pollarded willows there stood in water, and though the houses had never been flooded it smelled of the river and the walls were damp to the touch. Most of the houses on the estate were well looked after, with neat gardens. Only the Llewellyns, tinkers who had a huge number of children all with lousy, matted hair, had a house in a worse state than theirs. Although his mother complained about the Llewellyns, the piles of scrap in the back yard, the wild and smelly children, Laurie thought she was secretly pleased that they were there. It would have hurt her pride immensely if she had had the untidiest garden in the street.

At the end house in the crescent he stopped and opened the door with his own key. The house had been his grandmother's and even after her death was too small for the family. There was a smell of polish and vegetable and fried food so familiar that it smelled only of home. His mother had just come in from work and was sitting on one of the low chairs in the lounge, rubbing her legs which were swollen and marked with varicose veins. She had been busy at Gorse Hill, and it was all standing. Besides her usual work Mrs Masefield had ordered special cakes for the Open Day. Then she had had to walk back to town. She had a wide face and her eyes were narrow so she looked Mongolian or perhaps like a fat Eskimo. She looked very tired. He sat on the arm of the chair and put his arm around her shoulder.

'Make me a cup of tea,' she said.

'Where are the others?'

'I don't know,' she said. 'I can't keep track of you all. Steve is in, I think.'

There were seven children, five still at home. They had all done well. They were a credit to her. Even when their father was still at home the responsibility for raising them was hers alone. Paul and Tony had good jobs, Laurie and Heather had better than average reports from the high school, Carol and Michael, still in primary school, were polite and well-behaved. Only Steve was unemployed. He was her favourite, a worry to her.

Laurie went into the kitchen to make the tea. He was tempted to ask her if she had heard from his father, but he knew it would only worry her and make her suspicious. It was a coincidence, he thought. He was being silly. The van had been clapped out years before when his father left. It wouldn't still be going now.

She shouted to him from the living room. Her voice was still different from theirs. She had been born in Sarne and kept the border accent with its hint of Welsh all the time she was away. They still spoke Black Country like their father. They had lived in Wolverhampton, where his work was, until their mother had decided she could tolerate him no longer and they had moved back to live with Grandmother.

'What have you been doing today?' she shouted, a trace of accusation in her voice. 'You promised you'd mend that back fence.'

He poured out the tea and carried a cup in to her.

'I went for a walk,' he said lamely. 'I'm sorry.' He did not want to tell her about Helen. He could imagine her sneering disapproval. She thought the girls at Gorse Hill were lazy and spoilt.

'You'll have to do it tomorrow,' she said. She was angry. He was old enough to be working, to be bringing in a wage. He took his freedom for granted.

'Not tomorrow,' he said. 'I'm playing at the Open Day at Gorse Hill.'

'You should help more,' she said, the tiredness making her petulant. 'I can't be expected to do it all.'

'You should ask Steve,' Laurie said, stung at last by the injustice of her criticism. 'He's at home all day.'

'It's not his fault he can't find work.'

She drank her tea, sighed, and the disagreement hung between them.

The door opened and Heather came in, bright and unaware of any tension. She had a Saturday job in a café in the town. She was carrying a wicker basket full of pies and cakes and bread which would be too stale to sell on Monday. She was reliable, good-natured, with her father's dark hair and eyes.

'No need to cook tonight, Mom,' she said. She took the basket into the kitchen and immediately started laying the table there for tea. 'I saw Carol and Michael on the swings. I told them to come in for their tea. I don't know what Mike's been doing. He's filthy. I'll put him in the bath after.'

It's not fair, Laurie thought. She's fourteen. She should be out enjoying herself on a Saturday night, not looking after them all. I should help more. Steve should help more.

The younger children ran in from the street, squabbling, their voices still pitched for the playground. The door banged behind them. They turned on the television. It was very noisy – the plates banging in the kitchen, the children's voices, the television. His mother sat in the middle of it, still rubbing her legs.

'I'll take a cup of tea up to Steve,' Laurie said, hoping to restore himself to his mother's favour and to escape the chaos. He would have liked peace, time alone, to think of Helen.

Steve was in their bedroom, listening to a tape on the stereo system their father had bought them one Christmas in a last desperate gesture to buy their affection or at least to pay for their complicity in his absences.

'That's a new tape,' Laurie said. He sat on his bed, put the cup of tea on the window sill. 'I thought you were broke.'

'I was.'

Steve was only a year older than Laurie and they understood each other. Laurie had made the observation about, the tape casually but something about Steve's reaction made him press the point.

'Where did the money come from?' he asked.

Steve shrugged. He pulled four ten-pound notes from his jeans pockets and pushed one towards. Laurie.

'Dad's back,' he said. 'He gave it to me.'

Laurie was not as surprised as he should have been. It seemed now that the whole day had been leading up to the news of his father's return.

'You should give it to Mum.'

'It's payment,' Steve said aggressively. 'I'm going to work for Dad.' Of all of them. Steve had been the most, willing to believe their father's stories and accept his presents.

'What sort of work?'

'I don't know. It hasn't started yet.'

'Where's Dad staying?'

'How should I know?' Steve stood up, his hands thrust into his pockets. Laurie knew he was lying. 'He's promised me money,' Steve said. 'Lots of money. It's nothing to do with you.'

He raged out of the house without telling his mother where he was going and did not return until Laurie was asleep.

In the comfortable disarray of her room Fanny lay on her stomach on the unmade bed and watched a game show on the portable television. Her parents had bought the television to prevent some of the arguments between Eleanor and Fanny and now the child spent most of her free time in her room. She preferred children's cartoons but would watch anything.

Although Fanny had pretended that she was unmoved by Eleanor's public rebuke for eating cakes from the kitchen, she brooded about the episode. It was just like her grandmother to cause a scene to make her look small. What a fuss about a couple of meringues! She would never have known if Mrs Oliver hadn't gone to her, telling tales.

The incident had made Fanny more determined than ever to have nothing to do with the preparations for the Open Day. She would not be seen to help Eleanor in any way. It seemed especially unfair that the event was to be held on a Sunday – the only day that she had her parents to herself. On Sunday afternoons the three of them would go out together in the car. If it was fine they would go for a walk – not a long walk because Fanny disliked rigorous exercise – then they would stop somewhere for tea and Fanny could eat as many cakes as she wished without Eleanor staring disapprovingly at her. Even her father, usually so quiet and formal, let his hair down on Sunday afternoons and told jokes like other people's dads. She liked to pretend that she was nearly adult but the Sunday-afternoon treat was a return to the security of her childhood before Gorse Hill, when nothing mattered to her parents but her own happiness. She longed passionately for a time without her grandmother.

Silly old cow, she thought bitterly. I wish she'd drop dead.

Chapter Two

That evening dressing for dinner George felt an old adolescent excitement. It had something to do with Gorse Hill. During the tedium of his childhood Gorse Hill had represented glamour and sophistication and an escape from the town. At these times his picture of the house was always the same. It was always winter and a clear, frosty night. All the windows of the house were lit and inside the owners were holding a party. On the still air he could hear music and women's voices. Large cars drew up outside the house and laughing, well-dressed couples ran up the steps and disappeared inside. In these dreams George was always outside, unseen, looking in. He was sure he had never been present on an occasion like that – as a child nothing exciting ever happened to him and he was never allowed out at night. He thought the picture came more from 1930s Hollywood than from real recollection, but the scene dramatized his image of Gorse Hill at the time he was living at Sarne and he half hoped every social event there would have the same glamour and starlit quality. So his excitement had something to do with his romantic picture of the house. But it had more to do with Eleanor, with her elegant body and her perfume and the vague promise of intimacy.

Molly had dressed in a Laura Ashley skirt and blouse which her daughter had bought at a sale then grown out of. As a concession to the occasion she had put on a pair of evening shoes with a small heel, but she wore them rarely and was unused to them. They made her walk awkwardly and drew attention to themselves so she seemed to have very large feet. She was sitting at the dressing table in their bedroom wondering if she dared try some make-up. She had done her best to conform to the occasion and as he watched her across the large room George thought she looked like a teenager preparing for her first party. He felt an amused, rather patronizing affection for her. Throughout the evening it would be Eleanor Masefield who would hold his attention.

They dined together late when all the other guests had finished. Richard and Veronica sat on one side of the table, he and Molly at the other, and Eleanor dominated them at the head. Helen served them. Eleanor said little and though she welcomed them with suitable pleasure she was so subdued that he wondered if she were ill or tired. George thought he had never seen her so beautiful. He was aware of every movement she made. He was breathless, trembling with admiration. She had a ballerina's build and grace and fine features. She was tiny. She wore soft grey hair away from her face, a plain cream dress and a smile which made it clear she found him attractive. Beside her the other women at the table seemed bloated and uninteresting.

'Well then Eleanor, what's all this about?' he asked. He realized that he sounded like a hearty family doctor and continued, trying to make his voice more businesslike: 'What exactly do you want me to do?'

'I don't know,' she said and that surprised him, because Eleanor always knew her own mind and even if she were undecided she would never admit it. She must have sensed his surprise because she smiled at him. 'Give me time, George,' she said. 'I'm so tied up with this Open Day tomorrow that I can't think straight about the peregrines until it's over. There will be so many people here tomorrow that they can't possibly be in danger. Enjoy the weekend first and we'll make some definite plans on Monday morning.'

'But it seemed so urgent on the phone,' he said, rejected.

'Yes,' she said. 'Things have rather changed since then.' She smiled again but her voice was firm. 'I'm sorry, George. I really can't discuss it now.' She touched his hand and in the pressure of her fingers he felt she was asking him to forgive her secrecy, her feminine inconsistency.

The notion that she was in some personal trouble came to him again and he would have persisted, but she changed the conversation and was so sparkling and intelligent that it seemed to him that the evening had some of the magic of his dream.

As soon as the meal was over Eleanor left them, without apologizing.

'I'll be in the office for the next hour, Richard,' she said. 'Perhaps you could come to see me later so we can complete the arrangements for tomorrow.'

With Eleanor's departure the mood of the evening changed. They sat uneasily round the table drinking coffee. The rest of the room was dark and quiet. No one seemed willing to pick up the thread of the conversation.

'What did you mean,' George asked Veronica abruptly, 'when you said your mother seemed mad?'

Veronica glanced briefly at her husband. He thought her anxiety about Eleanor was misplaced. Eleanor was a tough old boot, he said. She probably had her own reasons for making such a fuss about the birds. But his long, mild face gave nothing away.

'She's obsessed with the peregrines,' Veronica said. 'She wandered about on the hill at night because she says someone's planning to take the young. No one else believes her: I don't know what to do.'

'Why does she think someone's planning to steal the birds?' Molly asked. She had been quiet all evening. The dinner had been Eleanor's show and she had not wanted to spoil the performance. Now she, at least, felt more comfortable.

'It's ridiculous,' Veronica said. 'There was a blue van parked at the end of the lane by the barn and Mother was convinced that it belonged to people who were looking for the nest. There was no reason at all why it should have done.'

'Did she get the registration number?'

'Not in detail. She just recognized that it wasn't a local one. When she first mentioned the van she didn't seem too worried by it but it seemed to prey on her mind so that now she's got the whole thing out of proportion.'

'She didn't seem very eager to discuss it tonight,' Molly said.

'No,' Veronica said. 'That just shows how illogical the whole thing is.'

'Did anyone else see the van?' George asked.

Veronica shook her head. 'No,' she said. 'The second time Mother saw it she came in and told me. She said there was a man sitting in the passenger seat. I was going to find out who he was and ask what he was doing there, take down the registration number, but when I got out no one was there. The van must have driven away.'

Throughout this conversation Richard Mead was silent. He gave the impression of scepticism, as if he wanted to reassure his wife that Eleanor was as strong as she had always been.

'I shouldn't worry about Eleanor,' he said. 'She's never struck me as the sentimental sort and I'm sure she's perfectly sane.'

He stood up, gave them his lopsided smile. 'I'd better go,' he said. 'She'll be expecting me.'

Veronica watched him leave the room with a kind of desperation, as if he too were deserting her. She sat for a few minutes longer, then she left them too.

That night George went to bed with the unsettling, unreasonable depression which troubled him occasionally. He felt that Eleanor did not trust him. His pride was hurt because he had driven all the way to Herefordshire to help her and she had treated him like one of the paying guests. The promise of the evening was unfulfilled.

When she left the dining room Veronica Mead went straight upstairs by the back staircase from the kitchen. She was confused and unhappy and did not want to meet any of the guests. She would go in to the girls, she thought, and settle them for the night as she had when they were babies. The idea gave her some comfort. The Meads had a series of rooms on the top floor. Once they had been used as a nursery and servants' quarters, but that had been long before Veronica had been born. Now they were airy and attractive and formed a retreat from Eleanor and the hotel.

Helen was still up, dressed in night clothes, sitting at her desk writing.

'Oh darling,' Veronica said, impressed by her elder daughter's academic dedication. 'It's too late for homework.'

'It's not homework,' Helen said, 'but I'm going to bed now.'

She's changed, Veronica thought. She's grown up. She takes after her grandmother, not me. Everything's changing.

Fanny was asleep on a crumpled bed, surrounded by soft toys and pop posters. Veronica straightened the duvet and stroked her forehead. She felt a routine easy guilt. It was their fault Fanny was so difficult. Eleanor was right. She was too muddled and incapable to organize time for her family. We're alike, Fanny and me, she thought. We're both failures. Then she shut the bedroom door and forgot the girl, as if she had done duty enough by feeling guilt.

In her own room Veronica sat and looked at her reflection in the mirror. I'm weak, she thought. I let things happen to me. I'm not clever enough to stand up for myself. She knew she was too dependent on Eleanor but could do nothing about it. Even after her marriage she had needed her mother. In one sense their life together as a family in the flat over Richard's studio had been the happiest time of her life, but she had missed her mother's support and advice. She had persuaded Richard to move back to Gorse Hill and to join in the hotel venture.

'She'll dominate you again,' he had said. 'She'll rule your life for you.'

But that, after all, was what Veronica had wanted.

So now Eleanor's peculiar behaviour was like a threat to her own precarious stability. She needed her mother to be sane and decisive. She would rather be alone than face the mood swings, the uncertainty of her mother's behaviour, the haunted look on her face, the night-time prowls on the hill. Richard was trying to protect her, to laugh away Eleanor's irrationality, but she knew something was going on which she could not understand. She could not explain her fears to George Palmer-Jones. He was obviously charmed by her mother, as most men were, and could not contemplate her madness.

There were footsteps on the stairs outside, Richard came into the room and Veronica turned round to face him.

'How was Mother?' she asked. 'She seemed quite well at supper.'

Richard shrugged and Veronica thought: He won't tell me the truth. He's afraid of hurting me.

'She was well enough,' he said. 'She didn't talk about the birds at all tonight. She wants the Open Day to be a magnificent success. Just like old Eleanor.'

He smiled but she knew he was lying.

The next day Helen woke early, but there were already people in the garden, setting up trestle tables, marking out the sites for stalls. She heard her grandmother's voice and saw Eleanor standing on the lawn, showing vans and cars and people where to go. She was dressed in brown trousers and a shirt and her hair was tied up in a scarf. She was waving her arms and shouting and might have been the director of a film. Helen dressed and ran down into the garden to offer help. She admired her grandmother's energy and wanted to be part of the proceedings. She thought it would make the time pass quickly before she saw Laurie again.

It would be another fine day, even warmer than the previous one. She felt happy, optimistic. Even when the heavy dew on the grass soaked her shoes she did not care. It was going to be a brilliant day. She stood where her grandmother had instructed under the cedar tree on the front lawn and checked the people who were running stalls against a list. When a dark, insignificant man got out of a blue van and said he was there to work for Mr Fenn, she smiled at the coincidence of the vehicle but took no real notice. There were a lot of blue vans and everyone knew her grandmother was making a fuss about nothing.

Helen was outside all morning and watched with wonder as the scene took shape. This was going to be no glorified jumble sale. Eleanor had planned something more impressive than that. There were to be displays of crafts, a sheepdog trial, morris dancers. There was an inflatable for the children to bounce on and a Punch and Judy for them to watch. There were ice cream vans and hot-dog stands and bands and balloons and a parade of vintage cars. The colour and noise suited Helen's mood exactly. She was reading *Le Grand Meaulnes* for A level French and the carnival music, the children in fancy dress, the friendliness of the participants reminded her of the party at Augustin's secret domain.

The event was opened at two o'clock by an actress more famous for her involvement with the Green movement and for her refusal to wear fur coats and leather shoes than for any of the roles she had played. No one knew how Eleanor had persuaded her to come but her presence at the event had generated a lot of publicity and the makeshift car park in the field across the lane was full. The large gardens were heaving with people. Helen listened to the opening speech and waited for Laurie's arrival in a state of breathless unreality. The scene around her was fiction, art, only a backdrop for their meeting. Soon she would see him and the whole purpose of the day would be realized.

The singers and dancers were performing in a corner of the garden furthest away from the house and Helen made herself wait until the speeches were over and the applause had faded before going to find Laurie. There was no stage. The musicians played on a square grass court and the audience sat on shallow grassy terraces which formed three sides of it. That part of the garden was sheltered and very hot, and not so crowded as the rest of Gorse Hill. At first she could not see Laurie. She looked through the people lazing in the sun and she was quite sure he was not there. A folk group were singing sea shanties and two children, showing off, were dancing barefoot, between the musicians and the audience. They were golden-haired, dressed in white frocks with blue sashes and they stopped every now and then to collapse in a fit of giggles. Helen turned to find somewhere to sit and then she saw him. He was coming back from the beer tent, walking across the grass towards her. He was carrying a drink. It was cider, he said. For her. He had to go now. It was his turn to perform.

The sea shanties were over. The musicians bowed and the little girls ran away still giggling. Laurie sauntered down the grass slope and took his place. She watched him over the rim of her glass and he smiled at her. He bent over his guitar. As he played the introduction to his song she could only see the top of his head with its stiff wiry curls, and his fingers. The nails were bitten so low that the brown stubs of his fingers looked unusually soft and round. Later she would not remember the tunes he had played, though she listened with rapt attention. His voice was light and melodic. She could tell that the rest of the audience enjoyed his songs and she felt proud of him and wanted to tell them that he belonged to her.

When he finished singing he came back to her with more drink – beer for himself and cider again for her. She had hardly tasted the first glass. He sat beside her on the grass. She turned towards him and kissed him. When it was over and she opened her eyes she saw Eleanor standing on one of the terraces opposite, staring at her with steely disapproval. Helen blushed but with an attempt at defiance pretended not to notice. She kissed Laurie again and when she next looked Eleanor had disappeared.

She had thought they would spend the afternoon there, in the sunshine, as they had on the hillside the day before. She wanted to show him round Gorse Hill, to take him to all the favourite places. She thought they might even walk on to the hill again and sit under the boulder so that they could be alone. But after ten minutes Laurie said he had to go. There was someone he had to meet.

'Who is it?' she asked. She was confused by the sunshine and the cider. She thought he would come back to be with her for the afternoon.

'Oh,' he said with contrived irony. 'No one important. Only my father.'

She wanted to ask him to explain. She knew his father had left them, that his parents were separated. She wanted to ask if she might go with him. But he got quickly to his feet, kissed the top of her head and ran up the grass slope away from her. She wanted to call after him to ask when she would see him again, where they would meet, when he had seen his father, but there was nothing she could do. He had disappeared into the crowd.

Irrationally she blamed Eleanor for Laurie's disappearance. She felt foolish, despised, as she had when she had opened her eyes and seen Eleanor staring at her. Her grandmother should not have pried on her. What right had Eleanor to follow her and disturb them in their private moment of pleasure? Miserable and wretched, because Laurie had not confided in her and had run away, she wandered off.

George woke late but still felt tired and edgy. The noise and good humour of the Wildlife Trust members who were setting up the stalls did nothing to improve his temper. Molly in contrast seemed more relaxed and comfortable. She was back in her old trousers and gym shoes and her confidence had returned. She smiled at the other guests.

Mrs Oliver served them breakfast. She looked flushed and angry, and when she brought coffee she spilled it into the tray.

'I'm sorry,' she said, though she was not sorry at all. 'I'm not used to this. I belong in the kitchen.' Her resentment was directed at George and Molly. It might have been their fault.

'I suppose everything's disorganized today,' Molly said gently.

'Mrs Masefield's stolen all my staff,' Mrs Oliver said shortly. 'I can't be expected to work properly with all this going on.'

She nodded towards the long windows. They could see the chaos on the lawn, the streamers and the noisy young people. She seemed to view the proceedings with a deep, puritanical suspicion. The participants were feckless, rowdy, and were disrupting her routine.

'I'll be glad when it's all over,' she said, 'and everything's back to normal.'

George was inclined to agree with her. Lunch was a scrappy affair but the other guests seemed to be enjoying the informality and shouted to each other with comradely good humour. He felt priggish and straitlaced. He would have preferred to remain in his room reading a bird book but Molly dragged him out into the crowd.

She began to enjoy herself for the first time that weekend. There was the noise and the smell of a fairground in a small country town. Someone had brought a fairground organ and the grating rhythm of the machine was interspersed with the music of the high school brass band. There was a smell of trampled grass and candy floss and frying onions. Molly thought that Eleanor might be

26

disappointed. Surely she would have wanted the event to be more refined.

Over the muffled public-address system came the announcement that the Puddleworth Falconry Display was about to begin.

'That's impossible,' George said softly. 'Eleanor must hate the idea of falconry. She can't have invited the Puddleworth Falconry Centre.'

He meant that he hated the idea of falconry and wanted to think that Eleanor shared all his ideals.

'Why not?' Molly asked. 'Wouldn't all the Puddleworth birds of prey have been bred in captivity?'

'But she's obsessed about her peregrines, neurotic about them. She wouldn't risk a falconer coming within miles of them.'

'She didn't seem very neurotic last night.'

He hurried away from her to watch the display. The aimless depression had disappeared. He felt there must be some significance in this latest diversion. Despite what Molly had said he found it hard to believe that the Puddleworth falcons had been invited to display there. Falconry was a legitimate sport and Puddleworth was a reputable centre with a history of captive breeding, but many conservation charities believed that showing birds of prey to the public encouraged the theft of raptors from the wild and refused to associate with the displays. George had visited Puddleworth as a Voluntary Inspector for the Department of the Environment and knew the director, Murdoch Fenn, well enough to be sure he would be recognized. He stood at the back of the crowd and watched the display.

The falcons and hawks were in a weathering ground roped off from the public. The hawks were on bow perches fixed into the ground and the falcons perched on wooden blocks. Each bird was tied to the perch with a leather leash which was fastened to the jesses on its legs. One by one the birds were taken from the weathering ground by Fenn to show off their skills. Fenn was a small, compact man with grey hair and a bank manager's moustache, but with a bird on his arm he gave the impression of strength and power. He took a peregrine first, unfastened the leash and allowed it to fly. Fenn was assisted by another man, as short as his employer but dark and slight. He held a long rope with a piece of padded leather at the end. The man swung the rope round and round his head, like a cowboy swinging a lasso. The peregrine circled above the man, following the leather lure as if it were a pigeon or some other small bird. The crowd watched the bird in silence, in awe of its power and control. The sun shone through the bird's outstretched feathers, the jesses trailed from its legs and the small bell fixed in its tail jangled. Men had been flying falcons in that way for centuries. Quite suddenly, it stooped on the leather lure as a wild bird would stoop on its prey. To the applause of the crowd Fenn retrieved the bird and fed it a small piece of raw meat. The peregrine was returned to the weathering ground.

The next bird to display was a red-tailed hawk, imported from America. It was larger and slower than the peregrine and flew lower, following the rope dragged across the ground. It too dropped on the imitation prey and it too was rewarded. It was a massive bird, built like a British buzzard but heavier with a wingspan of more than four feet. It had frightening talons, orange legs and a large curved beak. George supposed there must be some satisfaction in taming such a bird but he found the exhibition demeaning and the leather jesses on the bird's legs offended him, as would graffiti scribbled on the wall of a beautiful building.

George waited until the display was over and the birds had all been returned to their perches, then approached Fenn. He was unsure of the reception he would receive. During his inspections of the centre at Puddleworth, Fenn had been formal and polite but most falconers resented the intrusion of the Wildlife Act inspectors into their premises and George felt that Fenn was no exception.

'Mr Palmer-Jones,' Fenn said, shaking hands. 'I didn't realize the Department of the Environment were doing spot checks at displays.' He was formally polite but obviously hostile.

'It's not,' George said. 'I'm not working. I'm on holiday. My wife and I are staying at Gorse Hill for a few days. I was just admiring your displays.'

Fenn was obviously relieved but found it hard to make relaxed, easy conversation.

'Gorse Hill's a beautiful spot,' he said. 'I haven't been back since Stuart died. It's an hour's drive from Puddleworth but when Eleanor wrote and invited me to come I didn't feel I could refuse.'

'Eleanor asked you to show your birds today?' Carefully George kept his surprize from his voice.

'Yes,' Fenn said. 'I knew Stuart very well. He came to the centre quite often to photograph birds to illustrate his books – much easier naturally than trying to take pictures of birds in the wild. I became friends of the whole family. I was glad to come when Eleanor asked me. Publicity for our work is always useful.'

'Yes,' George said slowly. 'It must be.'

He walked to the weathering ground. The birds all seemed healthy and well cared for. All had the statutory Department of the Environment rings on their legs. Perhaps there was not such a contradition after all in Eleanor's attitude to Fenn. She could be determined that the peregrines on her hill should be allowed to live in the wild while admiring Fenn's skill with raptors which had been bred and reared in captivity. All the same he was disappointed in her.

While George was watching the falconry Molly walked on, past the other stalls, to the quiet corner of the garden where the folk singers were performing. There she saw Helen and her young man, lying together on the grass. They did not notice her. She was a shabby, elderly lady with cropped hair and schoolboy glasses, hidden in the crowd. Besides they would hardly notice anyone because they were so absorbed in each other. Molly watched the young people with pleasure and amusement. How intense they were, how happy and vulnerable! She watched Laurie run off up the slope and saw Helen wander sadly away in the opposite direction.

Molly did not follow Laurie. She was interested in people but did not have the sort of curiosity which needs to pry. She had been looking for George and saw the boy again much later, quite by chance. He was behind the row of poplars which marked the boundary of the birds' weathering ground and which hid the stallholders' cars and vans from the event. He was talking to a small middle-aged man. They were half hidden by a parked Range-Rover. They were talking in angry whispers and it seemed to Molly that the man just wanted the boy to go away. He was looking around him, so concerned that he might be overheard that he did not give the boy his full attention.

'Steve said you'd be here,' Laurie said.

'He had no right to say anything.'

'He thinks you're going to give him a job.'

'Carry on like this and you're going to lose me my job.'

'Leave us alone,' Laurie said desperately. 'We're all right. We don't need you now. Don't upset the kids again.'

'I'm not here to cause bother,' the man said. 'I won't come near the house. I won't try to see your mother. I'm here with my work.'

He had begun to whine and Molly could sense the boy's disappointment in the man who must be his father.

'Look,' the man said, 'I thought Steve might like to help me. I thought I could do him a favour. Just clear off now will you or you'll get me into trouble.'

'Dad ...' Perhaps the boy was preparing some gesture of reconciliation or understanding but the man turned away.

'I've got work to do,' he said. 'Clear off.' He set off with a rolling, swaggering walk down the drive, away from the house.

Molly watched him go through the gate and into the lane. The boy watched him too, then slowly followed.

Molly found George on the other side of the weathering ground. The birds had finished their last display and the area was quite empty of people. The birds were in a field invisible from the other stalls and it was very peaceful there. Fenn stood looking at his watch and frowning.

'My assistant's disappeared,' he said. 'I was hoping to leave soon. Have you seen Eleanor? I thought she might come to see me. I haven't seen her since this morning.' But he seemed not to expect them to respond and walked away to sit in his Range-Rover beyond the line of poplars. He tapped impatiently on the wheel, and looked at his watch again.

Molly and George went to the conservatory where Veronica was serving tea. It was late afternoon and the crowd in the garden was beginning to disperse. A snake of cars was winding down the hill towards the town. The conservatory was nearly empty and Veronica brought the tea herself. She seemed tired and strained but she kept up her bright chatter to the ladies of the WI who had been recruited to help her serve the pots of tea and plates of scones. They seemed able to maintain the thread of conversation despite the numerous interruptions as customers gave their orders, and George marvelled at the tenacity with which they pursued the gossip. Veronica set down the tray then hovered by the table, waiting until the WI ladies were out of earshot before asking:

'Have you seen Mother? I haven't seen her for ages. I was afraid she might have gone to the hill again to check on those blasted birds.'

Her tone was that of the school hockey team captain concerned about a wayward but respected member of the squad, but it seemed to Molly that she was very worried.

'I saw her earlier,' Molly said. 'She was watching the folk singers. That was more than an hour ago.'

'I expect she'll be back soon,' Veronica said. 'This afternoon's been a great success, hasn't it? She'll want to be here so the committee can thank her.'

Then she left them, and began to pile plates in an inefficient heap on the tray before Molly could decide whether any criticism of Eleanor was implied in the last comment.

Fanny had enjoyed the event much more than she had expected. In the morning she and her father hid in the office, like naughty schoolchildren, so Eleanor could not find them and bully them into helping her. Although her father was working, answering phone calls and writing letters, they giggled together whenever they heard Eleanor's voice, loud and clear travelling through the house:

'Has anyone seen Fanny? I need her to run into town for me. Where is that child?'

The office was at the back of the house and looked on to the hill. It was invisible from the gardens and they remained concealed.

This is how it should always be, Richard Mead thought. I should make more time for Frances. Eleanor ruined Veronica's life. Why should she spoil Helen's and Fanny's? His younger daughter had always been special to him. She had been a placid and smiling baby. He had taken photographs of her lying on a rug on the grass in the small garden behind his shop. He wished she never had to grow up. I'm only doing my best for them, he thought. All this work is only for them. One day the business will be theirs and they will have money to be independent.

Fanny lay on the office floor on her stomach reading a teenage pop magazine. She was not usually allowed into the office. It was Eleanor's special place. Although it was his work place not even her father was made to feel welcome. But today Fanny felt at home there and was happy.

After lunch her father had to take floats of change to the stalls administered solely by the Wildlife Trust. He winked at Fanny to show that although he was working for Eleanor now, he and Fanny were still allies. They shared the secret of their morning in the office. He asked if Fanny would like to go with him but she refused. It would be more fun to go to the kitchen to irritate Mrs Oliver. The game of annoying Nan Oliver had something of a child's dare in it because Fanny was frightened of Mrs Oliver, more frightened of her cold scorn than her anger. Sometimes the girl tried to win the woman's approval by offering to help to wash up, by baking a cake as she had been taught at school and showing it off. But the scorn remained.

'You're no help,' Mrs Oliver would say. 'You leave more mess than you clear up. If you were my daughter things would be different.'

So Fanny had given up trying to please and only went to the kitchen to make mischief. Today there was hardly any sport in the game. Nan Oliver, stony with resentment at the invasion of her kitchen, stood making sandwiches, surrounded by wire trays of scones and cakes. A big urn, borrowed from the cricket club, was hissing and steaming because no one knew how to turn it down.

When she saw Fanny, Nan Oliver gave her two jam tarts and an éclair to get rid of her. It had never been so easy. Eating the cakes, Fanny wandered outside.

It was all more fun than she had imagined. She soon forgot that she was a bored and cynical teenager and that she had resented missing her Sunday afternoon outing with her parents. Because she lived at Gorse Hill she was in a special position and she took advantage of it. She had free ice cream and candy floss. She played with the young children, laughing and rolling in the grass like a fat, overweight puppy. The whole event might have been laid on for her own amusement. Girls from school recognized her and envied her for belonging there.

Halfway through the afternoon, Fanny climbed the cedar tree in the middle of the lawn. She had not climbed it for years – she was too old for that sort of thing now – but she was happy and wanted to see the view from the top again. The tree was shaped like a green umbrella and from the inside near the trunk where she was climbing, she was hidden from the crowds. She and Helen had first climbed the tree on their Sunday visits to their grandparents. Even Helen had been unable to reach the top at first. It had taken weeks of practice, of finding a different way up. Each stage of the tree had been like a milestone in Fanny's growing up. She had been eight when she had made it to the top and pushed through the green foliage to be on a level with the top storey of the house and to see the gardens spread beneath her. She remembered their annoyance when two boy cousins had come to play. They had made it to the top on their first attempt without even following the approved route and made a nonsense of the seriousness with which the girls had viewed the feat. Of course Eleanor had disapproved of climbing trees.

Fanny climbed slowly. The wood was orange, flaky-barked and sweet-smelling. When she reached the top she was breathless. She had put on a lot of weight since she had last been up the tree. She sat in a fork in the branch and leaned back against the springy branches. No one noticed her. She could look down on them all. With surprize she saw the small figure of her grandmother moving against the crowd towards the entrance gate. Fanny wondered where she was going.

Probably to look at her silly old peregrines, she thought. She cares more about those peregrines than she does about us.

She watched her grandmother disappear up the lane and out of sight, then climbed down the tree and went to wheedle more money from her mother. But she could not find Veronica and by half past four she was bored and wished the thing would finish. She began to prowl around the garden, watching the final rituals of the afternoon – the prizegiving for the children's best fancy dress, the announcement of the raffle winner. Fanny was surprized that these were performed by the chairman of the Wildlife Trust and not by Eleanor.

That'll put the old cow's nose out of joint, she thought with satisfaction. She won't like that.

Then at last it seemed that the event was coming to its end. Fanny wandered to the field at the back of the house where the falconry display had been held. It was in deep shadow, crushed between the house and the hill. Beyond the line of trees on one side of the field, cars were parked and some were already driving away. As she walked round the house an old blue transit van passed her. It was going so fast that it scattered the gravel so that it rattled against the brick wall of the house. She turned her face away, afraid that a stone would go in her eye, so she did not see the driver. She thought nothing of it and walked on. It was followed by a lorry full of sheep which had been used in the shearing competition. In the caravan the morris men were changing into their ordinary clothes.

Beyond the morris men, in a Range-Rover parked close by, a man was asleep in the driver's seat, his head on his chest, so it almost touched the steering wheel. In the far corner of the field the birds of prey were still in their weathering ground on perches. Fanny went up to the rope which marked the weathering ground. The bird nearest to the rope was off its perch, though still attached to it by the leather leash. Fanny was so attracted to the bird, so held by its still, brown eye that she did not look at her grandmother immediately. Then she saw the silk pastel print of Eleanor's dress against the green grass, and the fine limbs jointed like a puppet's. She saw that the bird was perched on the woman's shoulder and had torn the fabric of the dress with its talons. The sharp cruel beak was pointed towards her grandmother's face.

She ran screaming to the man in the Range-Rover, hammering on the door and yelling to him that the birds had killed her grandmother and were pecking out her eyes. Then to her later, secret satisfaction, she fainted.

Chapter Three

George heard the screaming. When he reached the weathering ground a crowd had gathered round the roped-off area and were staring, fascinated, at the huge bird perched on the frail and slender body of the woman. The bird, sensing the attention, stretched its wings and turned its head. The woman's body was almost covered by the feathers. No one dared to approach the birds and a policeman, who had been at Gorse Hill to control the traffic, was clearly out of his depth.

'Let me bring the bird out,' Fenn was saying to him, his voice shaken and distressed. 'The woman's obviously dead. The red-tailed hawk couldn't have killed her look at her head – but it's a carrion feeder. It'll treat her as it would any other dead body.'

Fenn was a short man. He hardly reached the policeman's shoulder. He was white, almost incoherent with shock, and the policeman seemed unwilling to take him seriously. He was remembering rules about approaching the scene of the crime and the unwitting loss of evidence.

'For Christ's sake!' Murdoch Fenn screamed, an indication at last of his hysteria. 'If we don't move the hawk soon there'll be no body left for your pathologist to examine.'

He looked around wildly for a way to convince the policeman and saw George. It seemed to George that he was on the verge of breakdown.

'Look,' he said gratefully. 'There's Mr Palmer-Jones. He works for the Department of the Environment as a Wildlife Act Inspector. Ask him.'

Finally the policeman allowed Fenn and George into the enclosure and all the birds were put on portable perches in the back of the Range-Rover. The policeman cleared the people from the field, though by then the grass had been churned by their feet, and George thought there would be little to assist the forensic officers. Eleanor's body was left, roped off, as if the police had already been there and begun their work. As Fenn had said, it was obvious she was dead, but George, stooped over her body in a vain, childish hope that it was all a mistake. Her skull had been smashed, just above one eye, and though the skin was not broken the shape of her face was quite altered. He thought for a brief moment that it was not Eleanor at all but some other woman, then he realized he was deluding himself. He had known from the beginning that no bird could have killed her. Even if, as in some melodramatic horror film, the hawk had been trained to attack humans, Eleanor would have had no reason to wander into the weathering ground. Now the head wound showed that she had suffered no accident, no heart attack. She had been murdered.

He had always thought revenge a misguided and destructive emotion, but having seen Eleanor lying on the grass amidst the droppings, the dirty straw, the discarded pieces of fur and feather of the birds' prey, he felt angry and violent. She was beautiful, he had admired her and she had been killed.

He looked briefly around him for some smooth round implement which might be the murder weapon but there was nothing. He slipped away from the field and went into the house by the back door. He collected his binoculars and telescope from his room then joined the gossiping people who had been excited by the tragedy and were making their way down the drive to the lane. Mrs Masefield had had a seizure, some said. She hadn't been herself for some time. It was those evil birds, they said. They would frighten anyone.

As he turned away from the other people at the end of the drive he was surprized to find Molly beside him. It had not occurred to him to wonder where she was.

'Where are you going?' she asked. 'Shouldn't you stay here to wait for the police? They'll want to talk to everyone who was staying at Gorse Hill.'

'I want to go on to the hill,' he said. 'To the eyrie. I'll speak to the police later.'

He would have preferred to be alone. His anger persisted and he felt guilty too, and sorry for himself. It would have suited his mood to be alone on the hill, with the sun setting over the Welsh mountains, throwing long purple shadows over the heather.

'It won't do any good, you know,' Molly said. She was almost running to keep up with him. 'Brooding on your own up there won't bring Eleanor back. You're not eighteen any more.'

She knew him too well. He had been seventeen when a close friend had been killed in the war. He had spent a night on the hill. It had been a romantic gesture, a way of saying goodbye. She was right. He was grown up now, too old for dramatic self-indulgence.

'I'm not going to the hill to brood,' he snapped. 'I want to see if the peregrine young are still in the eyrie.'

'You think they may have been stolen?'

'Eleanor was convinced that someone was intending to take them,' he said. 'No one believed her. They all thought she was over-reacting. But if she came here this afternoon and caught someone in the act of theft, that might be a motive for muder.'

'She was murdered?' Molly said. Like most of the crowd she assumed Eleanor's death to be an accident.

'Yes,' George said shortly. 'She was murdered. But she wasn't killed where her body was found. There was no reason for her to go that close to the birds of prey.'

'You think she saw someone stealing the birds? Then the thief panicked and killed her?'

'It could have happened that way,' George said. His conversation with Molly was already forcing him to think more clearly and precisely. 'Though it would have been a long way to bring her body down the cliff. And why dump it in the falconry centre weathering ground?'

'To throw suspicion elsewhere,' Molly suggested. At the moment it was more important for her to maintain the flow of conversation to prevent George slipping into depression, than to think intelligently and constructively about Eleanor's murder.

'It was a dangerous way to go about it,' George said scornfully. 'With all those people there.'

'Not necessarily,' Molly said. 'If the murderer had transport. The field had been empty since the display and Fenn was asleep in his car. It would be possible to drive over the field to the weathering ground without anyone noticing.'

But George was in no mood to concede the point and they walked on in silence.

It was half past six and the heat had gone out of the day. There was a slight cold breeze. They had climbed the steepest point of the path and could look down over Gorse Hill. Smoke was coming out of one of the chimneys. In the valley there was the shadow of a cloud over the town so that it looked grey and distant, but the sun caught the red brick of Gorse Hill and made it warm and welcoming, more substantial and attractive than it really was. It alone in the surrounding countryside seemed to have life and vitality. In comparison the hill was dead. They walked on along the narrow sheep path.

They heard the peregrines calling before they could see the eyrie. The birds were circling about the cliff making a high-pitched hekking. The call was relentless, unending.

'It's the distress call,' George said. 'The birds have been disturbed.'

They walked along the sheep track which crossed the hillside until they could see the eyrie. Both birds circled above them and even with the naked eye Molly could tell the difference between them. The male was smaller, slimmer, greyer. The female was brown and heavy.

The eyrie was in exactly the same position as it had been when Stuart Masefield had shown George the site. In the birds' calls George imagined he could hear the man's manic laughter. He longed for the noise to stop. He screwed his telescope on to a tripod balanced on the narrow path and looked into the eyrie.

'Well?' Molly asked. She was tired and hot from the climb and leaned against the boulder which had hidden Laurie and Helen the day before.

'Someone will have to go down to the eyrie to check,' George said. 'But I'm sure the young birds have been taken.'

He slung his telescope over his shoulder and they walked slowly down the hill.

Eleanor was right, he thought, and no one would listen to her. She wasn't mad at all. He would never touch her now, never know her and be important to her. His anger returned, blinding and senseless.

There was a stile across the footpath where it led down to the town. As Molly was climbing it her foot slipped on a muddy step, she lost her balance and toppled backwards into a dry ditch. Mildly concerned and irritated by her clumsiness George slithered down the bank to help her up. Molly was unhurt. She stood up and brushed grass and leaves from her trousers. On the other side of the stile and separating the ditch from the open hill was a drystone wall. Molly was about to take George's hand so they could climb together back to the track, but something about his face stopped her. He was staring at the bottom of the wall. The stones were uneven and loose in places. In a hole at the base of the wall was a dainty shoe made of cream leather. Molly was reminded of the fairy story of Cinderella. She thought that she was always destined to play the part of the ugly sister.

'That was Eleanor's shoe,' George said. 'This is where she was murdered.'

Alan Pritchard was slumped in his chair, a can of beer in his hand, watching football on the television, when the telephone rang. He swore. It would be for Bethan, his wife. She came from Cardigan and her relatives saw Herefordshire as a strange and foreign land. They thought she needed daily phone calls to keep her in touch with home. Bethan was in the garden, trying optimistically to sunbathe, and the boys were away playing. The football game had reached a critical point. Pritchard shouted, hoping that his wife would come in and answer the phone, but there was no response and it continued to ring, drowning the commentary on the television.

Pritchard got out of his chair, his eyes still on the screen, and picked up the receiver.

'Yes,' he said. 'Pritchard.'

'Sorry to disturb you sir,' said a familiar voice. 'Something's turned up.'

He swore again, turned off the television set using the remote control, and listened.

Superintendent Alan Pritchard seemed young for his rank. Perhaps he was forty-five but he looked younger. On first acquaintance it was hard to understand how he had achieved such rapid promotion. He was relaxed, easygoing, almost flippant. He seemed to take nothing seriously. But those who knew him better described a streak of stubbornness, of ambition which made him stick with a case until he got results. He had a temper too which dragged his colleagues out of apathy as he roared around the office, shouting at them in Welsh, but they never knew if the temper was genuine or a practised technique to make them work and enhance his reputation as a character.

Alan Pritchard was known to be a great family man. He lived with Bethan and their four sons in a modern, ugly bungalow near the river to the south of the town. The river there was wide and sandy and the garden ran right down to the bank. The boys were always playing there, paddling and building dams. The garden was a mess, with bikes the children had grown out of, dens built in the bushes and deflated footballs. Inside there were dirty nappies in the bath and toys in the kitchen and Bethan big and blousy, feeding the latest baby and talking to her mam on the telephone. Alan loved it. He raged occasionally against the mess, the constant diet of take-away meals, the ruinous phone bills, but he would not have changed it. He would never have exchanged Bethan, wide and easy and laughing, for the nagging, shrewish housewives his friends described, or his boys for their soft, pink, well-behaved children.

When he arrived at Gorse Hill Pritchard thought he had come to a madhouse. He had received a garbled message about a woman who had been attacked by a giant bird. The thing sounded like a

41

grotesque practical joke and he could find no one to explain what had happened. He had not been told about the Trust's Open Day and the remnants of the event confused him. Most of the stallholders and visitors had gone, but there were upended trestles on the lawn and rubbish all over the grass. The scene-of-crime team had not arrived – Sunday was the worst possible day to get officers out – and the family were no use to him at all.

Richard Mead came to speak to him but was too concerned about his wife and daughters to talk much sense. 'Speak to George,' he said. 'He's a private inquiry agent, Eleanor hired him. He'll tell you what it's all about.' Then he had gone to phone a doctor because Veronica would not stop sobbing and there was nothing he could do to comfort her.

So when George returned from the hill Alan Pritchard was asking for him. He was less concerned about George's unofficial status than he might otherwise have been and was only grateful that in this confusion of birds and weeping women he had found someone who could explain what was going on.

They had their first discussion in the conservatory. They sat among the plants on white wicker chairs. It was warm and humid and quite quiet. It was an incongruous setting to discuss a murder, George thought, far too old-fashioned and genteel. They should have been a vicar and his curate discussing sermons over tea and thin slices of Victoria sandwich. But perhaps it was an apt place to talk about Eleanor's murder. It suited her.

'I don't understand any of this,' Pritchard said, breaking in on George's thoughts. He was big, round-faced. He had been a rugby player in his youth but he had drunk too much and put on weight. George thought from the beginning that Pritchard was a clever man, confident enough of his own ability and position to be informal, not to be worried about breaking a few rules, yet something about his manner irritated George. He seemed to have no sense of urgency. He was too detached. The policeman stretched in his chair and stifled a yawn. 'You'll have to tell me what it's all about.'

But George did not answer directly.

'Was Eleanor Masefield wearing both shoes?' he asked. 'I didn't notice. Perhaps I should have done. But I was looking at her face. I was rather upset.'

'She was only wearing one shoe,' Pritchard said.

'Then I know where she was murdered,' George said. 'At the end of the lane by the barn. Just on the other side of the stile on the hill there's a ditch. The other shoe is caught in there.'

He had expected some immediate reaction, a flurry of activity, but Pritchard did not move.

'Explain what you're doing here,' the policeman said comfortably. 'It might help me to understand the background to all this.'

Briefly and logically George explained his connection with the Masefield family, how his experience of working in the Home Office had led him to form the advice agency, the summons from Eleanor and her concern that the peregrine chicks might be stolen.

'I didn't have the opportunity to talk to her in any detail,' George said, remembering with regret their last meal together. 'The local Wildlife Trust held its Open Day here and she said she was too busy to discuss the peregrines until it was over. I presumed she was worried that some unscrupulous falconers were planning to steal the birds, either for their own use or to sell. Of course that's illegal under the Wildlife and Countryside Act.'

'Of course,' Pritchard said, and smiled. He was so relaxed that he might have been in the pub, a glass of beer on the table, discussing last Saturday's football match. George could not tell if he had even heard of the Wildlife and Countryside Act.

'I've been on to the hill,' George said. 'That's how I found the shoe. I'm reasonably sure that the young birds have been stolen.'

'You think the old lady was killed because of a few birds?' The policeman seemed to think it absurd.

'This isn't a matter of schoolboys climbing trees and taking thrushes' eggs.' George said indignantly. He did not like to think of Eleanor as an old lady. 'The birds can fetch a considerable sum on the international market. If Eleanor was suspicious, went on to the hill and frightened the thieves, isn't it possible that one of them panicked and murdered her?'

Pritchard shifted his large bulk in the uncomfortable wicker chair. It creaked dangerously. He seemed to be considering the matter.

'What made Mrs Masefield so convinced that the birds were in danger?' he asked.

'A blue van was parked at the end of the lane for a couple of evenings. She seemed to find that worrying. Her family thought she was making a lot of fuss about nothing and the people she contacted in the conservation business didn't take a lot of notice of her.' He paused. 'I had the impression that she knew something else but was too frightened to say. I thought perhaps she might be in some personal danger.'

'What sort of personal danger?'

'I don't know,' George said. He felt a little foolish. 'Perhaps I was making too much of it.'

'Perhaps,' Pritchard said. 'Tell me about these birds.'

'Peregrines aren't very rare, though these are rather special. They had sentimental value for Eleanor because her husband was so attached to them. Inland English sites are quite uncommon and there was a peregrine at Sarne in the sixteenth century. That might make the birds more valuable to an interested falconer.'

'And would . . .' Pritchard hesitated and looked at his notes to check the name '. . . would Mr Murdoch Fenn be an interested falconer?'

'No,' George said. 'Really it seems very unlikely. Eleanor invited him to come to the Open Day – she would hardly have done that if she thought he might be intending to rob the nest. His Falconry Centre is the most reputable in the country and I know his captive breeding programme is very successful. He would hardly need the birds himself and I don't think he'd risk his reputation by selling them. Besides, if he killed her on the hill it would surely be foolishness to put her body in the weathering ground where it would draw attention to himself.'

Pritchard thought again, deeply, with his eyes shut, then changed the subject.

'Tell me about the family,' he said. 'Would any of them have wanted to see the old girl out of the way?'

George wanted to tell Pritchard that he was being offensive, that he should not talk about Eleanor Masefield in such a dismissive way, but instead he considered the question.

'No,' he said. 'I presume that Gorse Hill will go to her daughter Veronica now, but I don't think that will make any difference to the Meads' way of life. They seemed to have a joint interest in the hotel. I suppose if Veronica or her husband had a massive debt there might be a motive for murder because Gorse Hill could be sold, but that seems unlikely. Veronica always seemed dependent on her mother and Richard Mead remarkably tolerant of his mother-in-law. There are two granddaughters and I had the impression there was some difference of opinion between them and Eleanor, but some friction would only have been natural.'

'So,' Pritchard said, 'It looks as if it had something to do with those birds.'

He stood up suddenly and George was surprized by the speed and agility of the movement. 'Stay there, sir,' he said. 'I want to make a few phone calls, tell my colleagues about that shoe up on Gorse Hill. Then I've got a feeling that you might be able to help me. I'll get someone to bring you tea. I'll try not to be too long.'

Still talking he went out through a white door into the house. Through the open door the house looked cool and shadowy and George felt inclined to disobey the order. He wanted a bath and something stronger than tea. But if he were to find Eleanor's murderer he would need the cooperation of the police, so he stayed, a respectable figure drowsing beside the potted palms in the evening sun.

Pritchard returned about half an hour later. He came quickly into the conservatory.

'That's all right then,' he said. 'I've been talking to a friend of yours from the Home Office.' He seemed impressed and regarded the older man with amused deference. 'He said you were sure to help me. In your capacity as a Wildlife Act Inspector, of course.'

'Of course,' George said. It was natural that Pritchard would want to check him out, but to get hold of a civil servant on a Sunday took skill and determination.

'You will help me?' Pritchard asked seriously. 'I don't know the first thing about these birds and they're obviously important.'

George got to his feet. 'Yes,' he said. 'I'll help you.'

Pritchard opened the glass door into the garden and stood aside to let George walk through first.

'We'll talk to Mr Fenn,' he said. 'He's still sitting in his car. We invited him into the house but he preferred to stay where he was. He says he's worried about his birds. One of my men has been keeping an eye on him. If he's got those young peregrines in his car he won't have had a chance to get rid of them.'

They walked round the house to the field. The weathering ground was screened from view and there were other cars parked close to the Range-Rover. George could hear indistinct voices from behind the screen.

Fenn was red-faced and indignant. When he saw George and the policeman approaching he got out of the car, slamming the door shut behind him.

'This is intolerable,' he said, stammering. 'I demand to be allowed to leave. Why have I been kept waiting in this way?'

The demand obviously cost him considerable effort. He was a nervous man who would dislike making a fuss, and he finished lamely: 'You see, my daughter will be wondering where I am. She's going away this evening and I promised to be back before she leaves.'

'You must phone her,' Pritchard said, all Celtic concern and solicitude. 'Just a few words with me and Mr Palmer-Jones and someone will take you into the house to a telephone.'

'This is terrible,' Fenn said. 'What was wrong with Eleanor? Someone said she'd had a heart attack, but I saw her head. I don't understand what's happening. This is like a dreadful nightmare. You must let me get back to Puddleworth.'

'She was murdered,' Pritchard said. 'Not here. Up on the hill. Now why would someone want to put her body near your birds?'

'I don't know,' Fenn said. 'I wouldn't have hurt Eleanor.' He spoke as if he were offended by such a ludicrous idea. 'We were very close friends.'

He was dazed now but less hysterical. The shock of the news that Eleanor had been murdered seemed to have calmed him. He answered Pritchard's question mechanically.

'Mrs Masefield wrote and asked you to give a display for the Wildlife Trust?'

'Yes,' Fenn said. 'She wrote to me. I was a friend of her husband's and I've always thought her charming. Perhaps if things had been different . . . I wanted to see her again. I wanted to help her.'

There was a strange dignity in his words. He was trying, George thought, to be a gentleman. It was a disappointing surprise to George to realize that he had not been Eleanor's only admirer. He felt a stab of jealousy as if they were in some way rivals.

'Did you know that a rare bird nests on the hill near here?' Pritchard asked.

Fenn did not question the relevance of the Sarne peregrines to Eleanor's death, but answered automatically.

'I knew about the peregrine eyrie,' he said. 'Stuart Masefield showed me the site when the birds first returned to Herefordshire. But peregrines are not rare in Britain. Not any more. I'd argue that it should be possible now for recognized falconers to take birds from the wild. The population could stand it.'

He was talking too much, George thought. His nervousness was causing him to repeat what was obviously a pet theory. It made him feel safe to hear the words he had spoken so often before.

Pritchard raised his eyebrows.

'Is that so?' he said. 'Did you know that the peregrine young were stolen this afternoon?'

'No,' Fenn said loudly. 'Of course I didn't know. I run a legal operation. I would never consider taking birds from the wild until the law is changed.'

He looked at the policeman angrily as if he had been tricked into his opinion about the peregrine population. George looked at Pritchard for permission, then continued the interview.

'You had an assistant during the display this afternoon,' he said. 'Where is he now?'

'I don't know,' Fenn said. 'I let him go off for an hour this afternoon when the display was over. He has relatives in Sarne. I haven't seen him since.' Despite the tragedy there was a trace of petulant irritation in his voice. 'He's always been unreliable. I went to sleep in the car while I was waiting for him and didn't wake until that child came and banged on the window screaming that Eleanor was dead.'

'So you didn't see anyone approaching the weathering ground?'

'No. Of course not.'

'I think,' Pritchard said, 'you'd better tell us all about this disappearing assistant of yours.'

'His name's Oliver,' Fenn said. 'Frank Oliver. He works for me at Puddleworth.'

'Does he own a blue van?' George asked quietly.

'Yes,' Fenn said, surprized. 'How did you know?'

George ignored the question. 'There was no blue van parked here this afternoon,' he said.

'No,' Fenn said. He looked unhappily at Pritchard. 'Oliver said the tax was out of date, and he didn't want to leave it here. He was afraid the policeman controlling the traffic might notice. He brought some equipment for me early this morning then drove the van away again. He was going to fetch it later this afternoon to take some things back to Puddleworth. As I've said he left after the display but he didn't return.'

'Did Oliver come with you from Puddleworth this morning?' George asked.

'No,' Fenn said. 'He came up earlier in the week. He had some time owing to him and I presumed he wanted to visit his family. I arranged to bring the birds up myself and to meet him here this morning.'

'Were you surprized when he didn't turn up this afternoon?' Pritchard asked.

'No,' Fenn said. 'Annoyed but not very surprized. Oliver's a law unto himself. I only keep him on because he's so good with the birds.'

'Knows a bit about falconry does he?' the policeman said.

'Oh yes!' Fenn was obviously impressed. 'He's a very experienced falconer.'

'Well, Mr Fenn,' the policeman said. He sounded very pleased with himself. 'You'd better give us a description of Mr Oliver and the names and address of his family in Sarne. It sounds as if we need to ask him to help us with our inquries.'

'I can't give you the address of his family,' Fenn said, 'but Mrs Mead will be able to give it to you. Oliver's ex-wife works in Gorse Hill in the kitchen. Mrs Masefield always said she was invaluable.'

Pritchard beamed. So Oliver had inside information. It was all he needed. The inquiry would be quickly over.

They persuaded Fenn to go into the house to phone his daughter while they searched the Range-Rover. Fenn would have liked to insist on being there but he did not have the strength to stand up to Pritchard's jovial good humour. He did as he was told and walked over the grass to the house.

The birds were quiet and hooded on portable perches in the back of the car. George listed the species – redtailed hawk, saker falcon, goshawk and an adult peregrine – and noted the numbers on the plastic cable tie bands on their legs.

'Red-tailed hawk and saker falcon aren't found in the wild in this country,' he said. 'They will have been imported under licence or bred at Puddleworth. The Department of the Environment will tell us from the numbers on the plastic bands. At least, they should be able to. I'm afraid they're not renowned for their efficiency.'

'What about the others?'

'They breed in the wild in this country and both species are regularly illegally taken. As I explained, as far as I know Murdoch Fenn has never been suspected of breaking the law and I'm sure they will have been legally bred in captivity. The Royal Society for the Protection of Birds has an investigations department. If Fenn has ever been involved in anything dubious the investigations officer would know. If you like I could ask him if he's heard any rumours . . .'

'Yes,' Pritchard said. 'You do that.' They continued their search of the car. There were no young birds. There was a piece of rope but it was not long or strong enough to let a man down the rocky cliff to the eyrie.

'We'll have to let him go,' Pritchard said. 'For the time being.' He turned to George. 'You'll be staying at Gorse Hill for a while, will you?'

'I don't know,' George said awkwardly. 'The family may prefer me to leave. I wouldn't want to intrude and I certainly wouldn't want to interfere in your investigation.'

'No question of that,' Pritchard said. He hesitated. 'I'll have to visit this falconry centre in Puddleworth. I was hoping you might come with me. I'm still not convinced that Fenn's not involved.'

'Doesn't all the evidence point to Frank Oliver's being the murderer?' George asked. 'His van had been seen on the hill during the week. His employment with Fenn would have introduced him to other, less scrupulous falconers, so he would easily find a market for the birds. He could have moved the body from the hill to the weathering ground in his van while Fenn was asleep, without attracting too much attention.'

'You're probably right,' Pritchard said easily, 'but Fenn could be implicated. If he wanted those birds it would be natural for him to get Oliver to do his dirty work.' He locked the Range-Rover and they began to walk back to the house. 'You will come with me to Puddleworth? We might find something there to lead us to Oliver.'

It took George a while to answer. He looked to an upstairs window where Helen stood and stared out across the garden in blank disbelief.

'Yes,' he said. 'I'll come.' Eleanor had hired him. He would see the thing through to the end.

Chapter Four

Laurie Oliver left the Open Day before it was ended. After his meeting with his father he wandered round the garden looking wildly for Helen, but when he could not see her he walked away. Like a child he needed instant comfort and he ran for his home. The confrontation with his father had humiliated and confused him. He disliked the man, yet felt hurt because his father had seemed indifferent to his presence. He wanted the security of the noisy house with the children playing and his mother complaining. He wanted to be sure of himself again. Even Helen was a threat to his confidence and he walked past the strangers on his way to the lane with his head bent, hoping no one would approach him.

He began to walk from Gorse Hill into the town. The makeshift car park was still full and cars were parked on the grass verge of the lane, but people were beginning to drift away. Several times he had to stand aside to let cars past, but it was three quarters of an hour later, when he had almost reached the town, that he heard the sound of a vehicle behind him and turned to see his father's blue van rattle round a corner towards him. For a moment he thought his father had followed him to apologize, to reestablish contact, but the driver hardly seemed to notice him and the van hurtled on down the narrow road, almost touching the overgrown hedges on each side.

He walked down the high street but saw no one he knew. The shop windows were empty and shuttered for the weekend, and there was no one about. When he arrived home the house, too, was unusually quiet. His mother was alone there. Heather had taken the children for a walk to the park, she said. His mother was ironing. The ironing board was in the middle of the living room and she stood behind it, firm and implacable, pushing the heavy iron over the household's clothes.

'I wasn't sure you'd be back yet,' he said. She usually finished early on a Sunday but it had been so busy at Gorse Hill he had thought she might be working overtime. He was glad she was back. She paused in her ironing.

'I told Mrs Mead I had to finish on time,' she said grimly. 'I told her: "I've got a family of my own to look after. This is supposed to be the Wildlife Trust's Open Day. Let them do their own washing up." Mrs Masefield would have had something to say but Mrs Mead let me go.'

She looked sharply at her son. 'What's the matter with you, then?' she said. She had realized immediately that he was upset. 'What happened?'

Although the plastic basket was still full of washing she stood the iron on its end, switched it off at the plug and began to wind the flex round the handle.

'Come on,' she said, already beginning to become irritated. 'Tell me what it's all about.' He had always needed more care than the others. He had taken up more of her time and the others had missed out because of it. They did not seem to mind – Heather said he was sensitive and she should be more sympathetic – but she thought there was something nervy and girlish about him. She wished he were more robust, for his own sake as well as hers.

He'll grow out of it, she thought. It's a stage he's going through. But she had been thinking that since he was five years old. He had sobbed every day not to be left at school, and he had clung to her as she tried to leave the classroom. He looked very similar now, drained and wretched, slouched on his chair. She wondered when she would make time to finish the ironing. She loved him of course but begrudged the interruption to her peace. She had a lot to think about.

'I saw Dad,' he said. 'At the Open Day.'

'What was he doing there?'

He could not tell whether the information was news to her. Her face and her voice gave nothing away. He had wondered if she had seen Frank at Gorse Hill, if he had been into the kitchen to see her. She left the ironing board standing and sat beside him.

'He was working for the bloke from Puddleworth.'

She nodded. She understood whom Laurie meant. During her marriage she had lived with Frank's obsession with birds of prey. At their terraced house in Wolverhampton, the small back garden which she had planned as a safe place for the children to play had been filled with aviaries and cages. She had lived with the rituals of breeding and feeding and flying. When they were first married Frank had been working for British Rail as a steward and the falconry had been a hobby like racing pigeons or growing leeks. Then he had come to the attention of Murdoch Fenn and had become a fanatic.

'So he's still working at Puddleworth, is he?' she said, almost to herself.

'I suppose so.'

'Well,' she said, turning back to Laurie. 'What did your father want?'

'Nothing,' Laurie said angrily. 'He said he was too busy to talk to me.'

'So?' she said. 'Wasn't he always too busy to talk to us?'

'He talked to Steve,' Laurie said, with a sudden flash of jealousy. 'He offered Steve a job.'

'What sort of job?' she demanded.

'I don't know.' Laurie was sulky, because mention of Steve would always provoke her to a reaction. 'He paid Steve fifty pounds.'

'Why didn't Steve tell me?'

'He might be your favourite,' Laurie said, aware that he was being childish again, but unable to help himself. 'He might be your favourite but he doesn't tell you everything.'

She seemed about to say something, but then they heard children's voices outside. They had been playing in the sandpit in the park and they had sand in their shoes, in their pockets, in their hair. They ran in demanding food and their mother's attention. They wanted to tell her all about it. Heather followed them, as excited as they were. She had heard in the town that Eleanor Masefield was dead. She had been pecked to death, people were saying, by one of the big hawks from Puddleworth.

'Is it true?' she asked her mother. 'What do you know about it?'

Nan Oliver shook her head.

'I don't know anything about it,' she said.

The police did not arrive to look for Frank Oliver until later. The two younger children were in bed. The police searched the rest of the house then insisted that Michael and Carol should be woken up so they could search their bedroom.

'What's he done?' Nan Oliver demanded, facing the police officers, her legs braced as they had been when she stood ironing. 'He's never been in trouble with the police. He's a bastard but he's always stayed within the law. I don't want those children woken.'

'We need to talk to him,' they said, polite, sympathetic, but becoming impatient.

'He's not here,' she shouted. 'What do you want to talk to him about?'

'Eleanor Masefield was murdered,' they said. 'We think he may have information about her death.'

'Not murdered,' she said quietly. 'They said in Sarne it was an accident. With the birds.'

She had no stomach then for the fight and let them go upstairs to search the children's bedroom. When they came down they would not leave. They sat on a sofa in the sitting room and stared at her. Dazed, Laurie and Heather watched them question their mother, and when one said: 'A cup of tea would be nice,' Heather got up to make it.

There were two of them, a man and a woman in civilian clothes. They had introduced themselves as they came in but Laurie never saw them again and did not remember their names.

'Divorced are you?' the policewoman asked.

'Separated,' said Nan Oliver.

'When did you last see your husband?'

'When I left him four years ago.'

'Did you know he was in Sarne?'

'Not until this afternoon. Laurence, my son, saw him at Gorse Hill and told me.'

'But you were in Gorse Hill this afternoon. Didn't you see him?'

'No,' she said, trying to keep her temper. 'I was in the kitchen all afternoon. I was busy. Didn't they tell you that?'

'When did you last have any communication with your husband?' the man asked.

'I've told you. Four years ago.'

'You haven't spoken to him on the telephone or written to him since that time?'

'I've written to him asking for maintenance,' she said bitterly. 'But I never had any reply.'

'You didn't tell him about a pair of peregrine falcons nesting on the hill above the hotel?'

She looked at the policeman as if he were mentally defective.

'I left him because of his bloody birds,' she said. 'What would I want to do that for?'

They seemed at last to believe her. The policeman turned to Laurie.

'Had you arranged to meet your father this afternoon?'

'No,' Laurie said.

'But you knew he would be at Gorse Hill?'

'I thought he might be.'

'What did your dad say to you when you saw him?' 'Nothing,' Laurie said. 'Just that he was working there and he'd keep out of our way. That's why I wanted to see him. To tell him to leave us alone.'

'How did you know he'd be at Gorse Hill?'

'My brother Steve met Dad in a pub in the town earlier in the week. Steve told me he was working here. When we left Wolverhampton Dad had a job at the Falconry Centre at Puddleworth. I knew there was a falconry display at the open day so I thought he'd probably be there.'

'Did he say anything else to your brother, to Steve?'

Laurie hesitated. He knew his mother would not want Steve implicated at all, but jealousy made him vindictive.

55

'Yes,' he said. 'He offered Steve a job.'

The police officers looked together at Mrs Oliver. 'Where is your other son?' the woman asked.

'I don't know,' Nan Oliver said wretchedly. 'He left here straight after breakfast. I haven't seen him since. But he's a grown man. He doesn't have to tell us where he spends his time.'

'Where might he be?'

She gave the names and addresses of some friends. At last they seemed satisfied and left.

Oliver's van was found parked that evening near the station in Shrewsbury but he and Steve seemed to have disappeared.

At Gorse Hill each of the women was isolated in her own room and seemed unable to receive strength or comfort from the rest of the family. Richard Mead scuttled between them with useless bursts of energy, but when they heard him coming they shrank away from the sound and pretended not to hear the tap on the door, the soft words of sympathy. It had become his main purpose in life to please his women and make them happy. Now it seemed he was a failure even at that.

Since he had met Veronica she had depended on him. His friends told him, when they first married, that he was infatuated with her and that soon the honeymoon would be over. He would realize what a mistake he had made. She was too young for him. She was silly. But the honeymoon had never ended and he was still entranced by her prettiness and her trust.

It had been no great sacrifice to sell the photographic studio, so that Veronica could move back to Gorse Hill to be with her mother. The only way to make a living was to do an endless round of tedious weddings and sentimental portraits of fat toddlers. There was only a limited market for the landscape and wildlife photographs he most enjoyed. He had not begrudged Veronica the lack of his own independence, but he hoped that she might recognize it as an expression of his love and be a little grateful. Now her rejection hurt him deeply. She seemed hardly to recognize that he was there.

In those hours after Eleanor's death he seemed to age. Molly was in the kitchen washing the cups and plates which remained after the Open Day, and it seemed to her that each time he returned from one of his forays upstairs, to persuade the women to eat, to drink, to talk, he seemed smaller, more grey.

'You shouldn't be doing that,' he said once, seeming to notice her for the first time. 'You're a guest.'

'I'm nearly finished,' she said. 'I'd rather be doing something.' She dried the last teaspoon and put it with the pile of cutlery on the draining board.

'What will you do about the hotel?' she asked. He had always been calm and practical. She hoped a discussion of immediate problems might help him.

'I've asked all the guests to leave,' he said. 'The police want to talk to them first, but they have all agreed to go tonight.'

'Would you like us to leave?' She thought that George would prefer to stay. She could tell he was already involved with the investigation. But if Richard Mead found their presence an additional strain they would have to go.

'I don't know,' Mead said. At first, when Eleanor's body had been found he had longed to be rid of the police, the spectators, the strange people wandering through the house and gardens. Now he was daunted by the thought of the family alone, fragmented in the big house. 'No,' he said. 'Please don't leave. Not yet.' He sat for a moment in silence, then stood up suddenly.

'I need a drink,' he said. 'Do you want one?'

She nodded. He needed the companionship of someone to drink with.

'Poor old Eleanor,' he said. 'She was a bossy interfering old lady, but I'll miss her. She had style.' They drank in silence.

Pritchard came into the room so quietly that they did not notice him until he was standing between them at the table.

'I wanted to tell you,' he said. 'That we've taken the body now.'

'I don't know what to do about the funeral,' Richard said. 'I don't know what arrangements to make.'

'Shall we leave all that until tomorrow?' Pritchard said gently. He sat down.

'We want to talk to someone called Frank Oliver in connection

57

with your mother-in-law's death,' Pritchard said. 'Does the name mean anything to you?'

Richard Mead shook his head. 'Nan Oliver works for us,' he said. 'Is he some relation?'

'Her ex-husband. He works for Murdoch Fenn, the falconer. We think Mrs Masefield frightened him while he was taking the young peregrines.'

'So she was right,' Richard Mead said. 'We all made fun of her and she was right all the time.'

'Did Mrs Masefield tell you how many young birds were in the eyrie?

'Two,' Mead said. 'There were two chicks.'

'You didn't see anyone strange in the house today?'

'No,' Mead said. 'But Oliver might have come in. At the end of the afternoon I was in the office counting the money for the Open Day, but I spent a lot of the day outside.'

'When did you last see Mrs Masefield?'

Richard thought. 'At the opening ceremony I think,' he said. 'I don't remember seeing her after that.'

There was a pause. 'I'm sorry,' Pritchard said. 'I'll need to talk to the girl who found the body. Your youngest daughter. Frances is it?'

'No,' Mead said. 'That's impossible. She's still lying in her room. She's very upset.'

'I'm sorry,' Pritchard said, 'but I'll have to talk to her. Mrs Masefield can't have been lying in that field for very long without someone seeing her. Your daughter may have seen something. We need to know. Of course you can be with her when we talk to her.'

Richard Mead looked around him as if searching desperately for a way to prevent the policeman from disturbing his daughter. His glance fell on to Molly.

'You come too,' he said. 'You were a social worker. You were used to this sort of thing. You can make sure they don't upset her.'

Molly felt awkward. It was none of her business. But she was curious too. She looked at the policeman. 'Is that all right?'

Pritchard shrugged. 'Why not? If it makes Mr Mead feel happier.'

In her room Fanny had stopped feeling queasy after the faint and was beginning to be hungry. She wondered what would happen about dinner. If she went down to the kitchen to find out her father would make a fuss. When there was a knock at the bedroom door she hoped it was her father again, with a tray of sandwiches and a glass of Coke, but this time he was empty-handed and he was followed by a fat man and the little lady who had been staying at the hotel. She looked at them rudely. She did not know what they wanted.

'Are you feeling better, poppet?' Richard asked, sitting beside her on the bed. She nodded. She wished he would stand up and talk properly. He was showing her up in front of these people, talking to her as if she were a baby. It was nice to feel him so worried about her, but not in front of strangers.

'This is Superintendent Pritchard,' Mead said. 'He wants to talk to you. Can you answer some of his questions?'

She nodded again. She was lying on the bed, fully clothed.

'I'll get up,' she said.

'Are you sure? Do you feel well enough?'

'Of course,' she said and swung her legs on to the floor. Her father helped her to her feet.

She sat on a window seat, by the long narrow window which was at the side of the house and looked down the hill towards the town, away from the lawns where the stalls had been set out for the Open Day. Pritchard sat on the stool by the desk where she did her homework. Molly stood in the corner, just inside the door.

'Can you tell me what happened?' Pritchard said. 'What made you go to look at the birds?'

There was nothing much else to do, she said. The stalls were packing up. She had seen one of the falconry displays and she had wanted to get a closer look at the birds.

'Did you see anyone else in the field?'

She shook her head. It was really boring, she said. Everyone had started to go home.

'Where was Mr Fenn, the falconer?'

'Sitting in his Range-Rover.' She treated Pritchard as a teacher, whose job it was to prise the answers from her.

'Did he see you?'

She shook her head. Then she added grudgingly: 'He was asleep. The car radio was on – I could hear talking – but he was definitely asleep. He was snoring.' She stifled a nervous giggle.

'So no one stopped you going right up to the weathering ground – the corner of the field where the birds were?'

'No.'

'Did you see a blue van, an old blue van, parked anywhere nearby?'

She thought. 'It was driving away,' she said. 'I saw it before I got to the field. It was going really fast.'

'Did you see the driver?' Pritchard asked.

'No,' she said. 'If I saw him I don't remember.'

'Then you went up to the rope and saw your grandmother lying on the grass near the big hawk?'

'Not straight away,' she said. 'I was looking at the bird. It seemed to be staring straight at me. Then I saw her.'

She turned away from the policeman and looked out of the window. She seemed very pale and Molly thought she might faint again.

'That's enough,' Richard Mead said angrily, jumping up from the bed. 'Can't you see she's had enough?'

But Pritchard remained seated.

'She's being very brave,' he said. 'And very helpful. I'm sure she can answer a few more questions.'

Fanny turned back into the room. 'It's all right, Dad,' she said. 'Really.'

'Did you speak to your grandmother during, the afternoon?' Pritchard asked. 'Did she say anything about going on to the hill?'

'I didn't speak to her,' Fanny said, 'but I saw her. I saw her go out of the front gate and up the lane.'

'What time was that?' Pritchard asked.

'I don't know,' she said. 'It was in the middle of the afternoon.'

'Where were you?' he asked. 'How did you come to see her leave the house?'

She blushed. 'I was at the top of the cedar tree.'

Pritchard stood up and held out his hand towards the girl.

'Thank you for your help, Miss Mead,' he said. 'I'm sorry to have disturbed you.'

She gave him a sudden beautiful smile.

Helen was so unhappy that she could not think clearly. She lay, self-indulgently miserable, her mind blank. It was not just that she was grieving for her grandmother, though Eleanor had always liked her and been kind to her. 'Helen will do well,' Eleanor had said. 'She's a worker.' The comments had usually been made in comparison to Fanny, and Helen had known she was the favourite granddaughter.

Helen had seen Eleanor's body. She had heard Fanny's screaming and had run with the others to the weathering ground and had shouted ineffectually in an attempt to frighten the bird away from her grandmother's body. She had seen her grandmother, so upright and dignified in life, lying in the mud, her dress crumpled and wrinkled above her knees. The huge and powerful hawk dominated the scene. Its talons pierced the woman's flesh and the beak pointed towards her eyes. So it was natural to be dazed and to want to erase the memory of the sight from her mind.

What was not natural, Helen felt, was to care more about Laurie's disappearance than her grandmother's death. Why had he deserted her? He must have realized that she would be devastated by Eleanor's death. She had made no definite arrangement to meet him but she had taken it for granted that she would see him before he went home. At the back of her mind there was the anxiety that there might be something suspicious in his failure to find her again. He had been behaving so oddly. That thought was so terrible that she refused to recognize it. She lay, half asleep on the bed, waiting for the pain to pass.

When there was a knock on the door she leapt up immediately to open it. She knew it was probably her father, but hoped Laurie might be there, that at least there would be a message from him.

She was surprized to see three people there – her father, the quiet little old lady Eleanor had invited to Gorse Hill, and a stranger. She stared at them for a moment, shock making her thoughts and responses sluggish.

'I'm sorry,' she said. 'Do you want to talk to me?'

'This is Superintendent Pritchard,' her father said. 'He wants to ask you some questions.'

'Yes,' she said automatically. 'Of course, I'll come downstairs.' She did not want them in her room. They sat in the conservatory. The conservatory was not really part of the house and she felt their privacy less violated there. Yet Helen realized that was ridiculous because the house was always full of paying guests. The police, somehow, were different and more intrusive. She sat opposite her father and thought how ill he looked.

'I don't think I can help you,' Helen said.

'Perhaps not,' Pritchard said, accepting her judgement seriously. 'But I'll have to talk to you. There might be something, you see, which you don't realize is important, which might help. Tell me what you did this afternoon.'

'Nothing much,' Helen said. 'I wandered round the stalls and the exhibitions, listened to the folk music.' She would have liked to mention Laurie, as if the sound of his name made him real, but she did not think he would want to be involved.

'We think your grandmother may have been killed by someone taking the peregrines,' Pritchard said. 'Did you notice a blue van parked by the falcons this afternoon?'

'Not this afternoon,' she said. 'But I saw a blue van this morning.' She had forgotten all about it. 'I was checking in the helpers. It was driven by a man who said he was Mr Fenn's assistant. I didn't realize then that Mr Fenn was the falconer. And I didn't think there was anything suspicious about the blue van. It just seemed an odd coincidence. I should have said something, shouldn't I? I should have warned Grandmother.' She knew she should feel guilty, but was incapable of feeling anything.

'You mustn't blame yourself,' her father said. 'None of us took Eleanor seriously about the peregrines.'

'Did you see your grandmother during the afternoon?' Pritchard asked.

Helen remembered Eleanor standing on the grassy terrace, watching her kissing Laurie.

'Yes,' she said. 'I saw her near the tennis court where the musicians were playing.'

'Did she tell you where she was going?'

'No,' Helen said. 'I didn't speak to her.'

In the following silence Molly cleared her throat then spoke shyly.

'You were with a boy,' she said apologetically. 'It might not be important but he might have seen something which would help the police. Perhaps you should tell us his name.'

Helen blushed.

'Laurie,' she said. 'His name's Laurie Oliver.'

There was a stunned silence.

'Do you mean Nan Oliver's son?' her father asked. She nodded, surprised by the reaction she had provoked. Pritchard signalled to the other adults to be quiet. He pulled his chair closer to Helen's. The two of them could have been alone in the room.

'Now then,' he said. 'Tell me about this Laurie. He lives with his mam, does he?'

He might have been a favourite uncle, teasing her about a new boyfriend.

'Yes,' Helen said. 'Just with his mother. His parents have separated.'

'Where does his dad live, then?'

'I don't know,' Helen said. 'I don't think Laurie likes him. But he was here today. Laurie said he was going to meet him.'

'And what did young Laurie say to his dad?'

'I don't know,' she said. 'I'd expected Laurie to meet me later but he must have gone home early.'

She began to cry.

Veronica was too ill to see them. The doctor had given her a sedative. Eventually the sobbing had quietened and she had slept.

The doctor had left instructions that she was not to be disturbed until the following morning.

The police were out on the hill until it was too dark to work. From his bedroom window George could see them, walking backwards and forwards through the rough grass. In the shadow they seemed so close that he felt he could call to them. He should be able to ask them if they had found anything of significance and they would hear him. He even imagined that he could hear the peregrines crying still and that they were blaming him for their fruitless attempt to rear young, for the loss of their offspring.

'Well,' Molly asked. 'What do you think? Is Frank Oliver the murderer?'

'I suppose so,' George said. 'Everything points that way.' He resented her breaking in on his mood. The irritation was a novelty. Although he had married Molly because she challenged him and startled him into new ways of thinking, he had been comfortable with her for many years. He had always thought he would have been pompous and dull without her, but now he felt disconcerted by her questioning. It occurred to him then that they should return immediately to the big untidy house where they were at home with each other. He no longer wished to be startled. But the romantic idea that he was serving Eleanor remained and he did not suggest it. Molly seemed not to notice his confusion. She hated his mood of self-pity.

'Pritchard seems a competent man,' she said. What right had George, after all, to stare out of the window and exclude her from his thoughts? They were partners.

Reluctantly he moved away from the window.

'Yes,' he said. 'I think he knows what he's doing. He wants me to go with him to Puddleworth tomorrow.'

'Why does he want to go to Puddleworth?'

'He thinks Oliver might not have been working alone. He's probably right. I think it would take at least two people to go down that cliff.'

'Don't the police think now that he recruited his son, Stephen, to help him?'

'Yes,' George said, 'but Pritchard seems to think it unlikely that Oliver planned the theft himself. He seems to have taken a dislike to Fenn. I think he'd like to find evidence that the raid was all Fenn's idea even if he had no part in the murder.'

'Will you go with Pritchard to Puddleworth?'

'Oh yes,' George said. 'I think I shall go. I want to see the thing through.'

You're too involved in this case, Molly thought. You've lost your sense of perspective. 'What would you like me to do while you're away?' she asked.

'You?' he said surprised. 'I don't think there's anything you can do.'

Chapter Five

Pritchard arrived at Gorse Hill at eight o'clock the next morning to collect George and take him to the Puddleworth Falconry Centre. He seemed well rested and refreshed, cheerful.

Pritchard drove north along country roads through half-timbered villages, where cottage gardens were filled with bulbs. It was another sunny day but there was a strong, westerly breeze which blew round white clouds over the sky and the lines of washing in the long back gardens. They stopped twice – once to allow herds of cows to cross the road, on their way back to the low riverside fields from the milking parlour, and then in Ludlow because Pritchard was starving and needed a bacon sandwich and a mug of tea.

Puddleworth was on the east side of Wenlock Edge, surrounded by open countryside but only three quarters of an hour from the centre of Wolverhampton. The village was pretty, with the same clean, preserved look as villages in the south-east of England. No cow would make a mess on the road here, the pubs were so smart that they would intimidate any farm worker in boiler suit and boots, and the village shop sold camembert, pâté and ground coffee. The houses round the green were freshly painted and tastefully restored. Most, George thought, would be owned by people who preferred to commute to work in Wolverhampton or Birmingham every day than live in the city. He could not blame them. He too had been a commuter. But there was something sad and sterile about the place. A group of farm buildings in the centre of the village was being sold for development and in a field nearby the bulldozers had already begun work on a small complex of detached executive homes. The residents of Puddleworth would be prosperous, respectable and hard working.

The Falconry Centre too had an air of affluence, of respectability. A high, white-painted fence surrounded the large grounds. It was clear that visitors were not allowed a view of the birds without paying their two pounds entrance fee. The car park was outside the fence and empty. A young, well-spoken woman in green wellingtons came out of the ticket office to tell them that actually the centre didn't open until ten.

'Who are you then?' Pritchard asked, staring frankly at the tight jeans and sleeveless vest. She had a long, tawny mane of hair, freckles and blue eyes. She stared back at Prichard with hostility.

'I'm Kerry Fenn,' she said as if Pritchard was hardly worth the effort of answering. 'Actually, my father owns the centre.'

'That's lucky then,' Pritchard said happily. 'You can tell your dad we want to see him. My name's Pritchard. Superintendent Pritchard.'

She left them on the car park side of the turnstile and walked away across acres of gravel.

'Spoilt brat,' Pritchard said when she was still within hearing. He watched her contentedly.

Murdoch Fenn insisted on accompanying them round the centre despite Pritchard's attempt to let them look for themselves.

'You're a busy man,' Pritchard said. 'Mr Palmer-Jones knows his way round. Just pretend we're not here.' But wherever they went Fenn was behind them, immaculate and resentful.

In fact the place was so big that George would have had difficulty in finding his way round and was glad of Fenn's presence. The centre had expanded since his last visit. The gatehouse led directly into a large, airy brick building which Fenn called the interpretive centre. A series of display panels explained the work of Puddleworth and the history of falconry. There were glossy photographs and professionally produced diagrams.

'Kerry works in here during the day,' Fenn said. 'She's very good with the schoolchildren.'

At the end of the building in a separate, smaller room was a collection of original paintings. The subjects were exotic and romantic, and had little connection with the English countryside. There was an Indian rajah with a peregrine on his wrist, a group of Arabs in the desert hunting bustards and a sheik on horseback holding a saker falcon. Fenn led them through a door back into the open air. The hawk houses and aviaries were built on two sides of a large gravel square. The interpretive centre and art gallery formed the third side. On the fourth was an open, grass weathering ground, with birds on blocks and beyond that a glass dome.

'This is our new hawk house,' Fenn said proudly. He seemed for a moment to have forgotten his resentment. He was so pleased with his new acquisition that they might have been knowledgeable and rather important guests. 'We keep our New World birds of prey in here.'

The dome was separated into six segments by glass walkways which met in the middle to provide a viewing gallery so that members of the public could stand with the enormous birds all around them.

'We've recently acquired a crested caracara,' Fenn said. 'We're very proud of it.'

Pritchard followed Fenn round the dome with childish enthusiasm and gave no sign of impatience.

'So you breed these things in captivity, do you?' he asked.

'Not here,' Fenn said, responding again to the interest. 'Most of our breeding is done in a special area, beyond that hedge, where our visitors aren't allowed, but we have one house where we can show the public the steppe eagles' nest.'

He took them into a large building about one hundred and fifty feet long, forty-five feet wide and thirty-five feet high. The door led into a narrow corridor with a window into the barnlike room beyond.

'That's a one-way mirror,' Fenn whispered. 'Of course we can't allow the birds to be disturbed.' The place had wooden perches and branches and in one corner the female steppe eagle sat on the huge stick nest.

'I think Superintendent Pritchard might be more interested in seeing the British birds of prey,' George said. 'That might perhaps be more relevant to his inquiries.' It seemed to him that this guided tour was a waste of time, leading nowhere.

'Of course,' Fenn said formally, obviously offended, but Pritchard seemed to be in no hurry and was gazing, fascinated, at the nest.

The aviaries where the British birds were kept were smaller and made of linked wire-mesh, with a wire-mesh roof.

'We keep the birds in individual flights,' Fenn said, and pointed out buzzard, goshawk, sparrowhawk and finally peregrine.

'Of course that's the bird that breeds above Gorse Hill,' George said. He felt he had to drag Pritchard's attention back to the inquiry. The policeman seemed to be treating the whole trip as a jolly day out.

'Beautiful thing isn't it?' Pritchard said.

George would have liked to say that the bird was much more beautiful when it was flying free over the hill at Sarne but said nothing. His comment at least seemed to have had the required effect because Pritchard asked to be shown the aviaries not accessible to the public where birds were breeding or in quarantine, and the tour of inspection was finally completed.

'Where do you keep all your paperwork?' Pritchard asked when they were at last back on the gravel yard.

'In my office,' Fenn said. 'In the house.'

'That's convenient,' Pritchard said. 'Perhaps your wife could make us all a nice cup of coffee while Mr Palmer-Jones checks that everything's in order.'

'My wife's dead,' Fenn said abruptly. 'A car accident. About seven years ago.'

'I'm sorry,' Pritchard said. He meant it and Fenn nodded in recognition of his sincerity.

'I can make coffee,' Fenn said, 'if you'd like it. And I'll show Mr Palmer-Jones into the office.'

The house was a long, modern bungalow, built within the fence but beyond a small copse of trees. It was like something he had seen on American television, Pritchard thought. The kitchen was huge and spotless. Fenn made instant coffee and carried the three mugs to his office on a tray. George was obviously not to be allowed to look through the records alone. Fenn unlocked the filing cabinet for George, sat in one of the swivel chairs in front of the desk and motioned Pritchard to take the other. In the distance through the trees they could see Kerry leading a crocodile of schoolchildren over the gravel from the interpretive centre.

Pritchard gulped hot coffee.

'Your daughter didn't go away in the end then?' he said.

'Pardon?' Fenn looked surprized.

'You said you had to be back last night so your daughter could go away.'

'Oh yes,' Fenn said. 'She decided not to go in the end. I was so upset when I got home that she offered to stay with me.'

'We've talked to a lot of witnesses now,' Pritchard said. 'You'll be glad to hear that you were seen for most of the afternoon. You wouldn't have had time to get on to the hill to kill Mrs Masefield.'

'Of course I didn't kill her,' Fenn said angrily. 'Why should I want to do that?'

'You might have wanted the birds,' Pritchard said. 'Henry VIII took his falcons from Sarne, didn't he? And history's very important to falconers. We learnt all about that in your magnificent exhibition. Those birds must be very valuable.'

'I wouldn't steal birds from the wild,' Fenn said.

'We know you didn't steal them,' Pritchard said. 'As I explained before, you wouldn't have had time to. But it seems to us very likely that Frank Oliver might have done. He's disappeared, hasn't he? So I want to hear everything you know about Frank Oliver.'

'He used to keep his own birds,' Fenn said quickly. 'I don't know where he got them from. They might have been taken from the wild. It was more common in those days . . .'

'What are we talking about?' Pritchard interrupted. 'What days are those?'

'I don't know,' Fenn said. He seemed uncomfortable. 'Perhaps ten years ago. He was working as a steward on the railway then. I met him through the British Falconry Society. At first I thought he was a brash, unpleasant little man, but he was achieving some wonderful successes with his birds even then.'

'What sort of successes?' This time George interrupted, looking up from the file he was reading.

'You must know that goshawk is very difficult to breed in captivity, yet season after season he was rearing young birds in the most primitive conditions in a hawk house at the back of his home.'

'Are you sure he was breeding the birds?' George asked. 'The Greenholme forest isn't far from here. He would have known where to find young goshawk.'

'I was suspicious at first,' Fenn said. 'In the beginning he may have been taking birds illegally, but really he had great skill at handling the birds. He almost seemed to communicate with them. He was the most natural falconer I've ever met.'

'So you asked him to come to work with you?'

'Not immediately. The Centre wasn't so big or well established then. It was a struggle to survive . . . All my savings had gone into the project and I would have been unable to employ him. But because he worked long shifts for British Rail he seemed to take a lot of time off. Perhaps he was not so conscientious about his work as he should have been. In any event he seemed content to spend all his time here as a volunteer and in the end he brought his own birds here.'

'I don't suppose you were very popular with his wife if he spent all his free time here.'

'I suppose not,' Fenn said. 'In the end she left him. Oliver seemed not to mind. In a way it was more convenient.'

'So he came to work here?'

'Eventually yes. It must have been about three years ago. I think he was probably sacked from his job with British Rail. He told me he was made redundant but I think he was probably sacked. The Centre was doing rather better then and I could afford to pay him a modest wage. I was afraid that if I didn't employ him he might go elsewhere. I'll admit that by then I'd come to depend on him. He had developed some marvellous techniques to manipulate imprinting.'

'What's imprinting?' Pritchard asked.

Fenn looked helplessly at George as if it were beneath his dignity to explain so basic a concept.

'All newly hatched birds develop a relationship with their siblings and parents, which is part sexual, part food dependent and part aggression,' George said. 'If birds are hatched artificially they come to regard humans as their role model. They act unnaturally then. Some vets even say the birds become psychotic.'

'And Oliver found a way of overcoming that problem?' Pritchard asked.

'Yes,' Fenn said. 'Oliver wore a glove shaped a little like a bird, and put the glove into the cage to give food or water. That way there was no human contact. The falcon even came to regard the glove as a potential mate and we were able to obtain sperm for future breeding programmes.'

George looked up from the papers he was reading with extreme distaste.

'Where did Oliver live?' Pritchard asked.

'He had a house in Wolverhampton,' Fenn said.

'So he did,' Pritchard said. 'My colleagues have found it for us. But it was a long way for him to come every day.'

'He didn't mind the travelling,' Fenn said quickly. 'He had that old blue van. He's had it for years . . .' Then when Pritchard continued to look at him with disbelief he added: 'There was a room here where he sometimes stayed, if he was working late or for some reason he didn't want to leave the birds.'

'Here?' Pritchard asked. 'In the house?'

Fenn seemed shocked by the notion. 'Oh no,' he said. 'Not in the house. It's in the building where we keep the birds in quarantine. It was intended originally for volunteers. Then Kerry decided she wanted to work here too so we didn't need any extra help.'

'You didn't show it to us when we were looking round earlier.'

'No,' Fenn said. 'I didn't think it was important.'

George was packing files neatly back into the cabinet. Pritchard looked at him and he shook his head slightly to show he had found nothing of significance.

'We'd better have a look,' Pritchard said, as if it were a routine chore. 'Then we'll go away and leave you alone.'

Reluctantly Fenn led them along a pleasant path through the trees to the Centre. Oliver's room was small, with two bunks on one wall and a small hand-basin on the other. Grey blankets were folded neatly on the bunks. George thought it was very similar to a British Rail sleeping compartment Oliver must have been at home there.

Pritchard lifted the mattresses off the wire-framed bunks and shook out the blankets.

'Has it been cleaned since Oliver slept here?' he asked.

Fenn shook his head. 'I don't know,' he said. 'Oliver saw to all that.'

By then Pritchard was on his knees, peering under the lower bunk.

'It's a bit dusty under here,' he said. 'Reminds me of home.' When he stood upright he held a small scrap of paper between his thumb and first finger. A series of numbers was written in pencil. Pritchard held out the paper so that Fenn could see it.

'Does this mean anything to you?' he asked.

Fenn shook his head.

'What about you, Mr Palmer-Jones?'

George looked at the numbers. 'Yes,' he said. 'I know what that is. It's the telephone number at Gorse Hill.'

They walked together slowly through the turnstile and towards the car. There was already a scattering of cars in the car park and in the gatehouse shop a few people were looking at the tea towels and mugs all printed with falcon heads. Another coach was pulling up with a group of schoolchildren hanging out of the windows. Kerry Fenn hurried out of the gatehouse to meet the new party, then saw the men and hesitated. She stood by the turnstile willing them to go. As Pritchard and George reached their car Fenn turned and joined his daughter, put his arm around her in a gesture of comfort and support. As Pritchard drove off George looked back and saw that the couple were still watching with relief as the policeman pulled out into the road.

'What did you make of that then?' Pritchard asked.

George was still thinking of the father and daughter, supporting each other, facing the threat of the inquiry together.

'Fenn's a lonely man,' he said. 'I remember his wife. He had some sort of breakdown when she died. Before that the falconry was a hobby. He was quite detached and academic about it. He wrote books about its history and gave witty after-dinner speeches. He had been a solicitor before he founded the Falconry Centre and he spoke rather well. Then there was the tragedy of his wife's accident and his illness and the birds seemed to take him over. I suppose that nothing else was important to him.' Like Stuart Masefield, George thought. The birds took him over too.

'Except his daughter,' Pritchard said. 'He had his daughter to look after.'

'Yes. I've never met her before. I think she was abroad when I visited before. They do seem very close.'

George was lost in memory of the lively competent man he had known before Lydia Fenn's death. Fenn had seemed to have regained his confidence and composure with the success of Puddleworth, but the second tragedy of Eleanor's murder had shattered his poise again. He admired Eleanor as I did, George thought. Now he really only has his daughter and his birds left to care for. I have my wife.

Pritchard was talking again, a little impatiently.

'I meant. . .' he said, 'what did you make of Oliver's having a copy of the Gorse Hill telephone number?'

'I suppose,' George said slowly, 'that Nan Oliver must have been lying and she had spoken to him since their separation after all.'

'Exactly,' Pritchard said. 'The Olivers don't have a telephone at home. The whole family seem more involved with Gorse Hill than I'd realized at first. Did you know that Oliver's son and Mrs Masefield's granddaughter are very friendly?'

'No,' George said.

'I thought your wife might have told you. She discovered that little fact.'

'No,' George said. 'She didn't tell me.' He felt suddenly guilty because he had excluded Molly and had so obviously resented her interest. He wished Molly were sitting beside him so he could hold her hand and make everything right. He wanted to tell her that his admiration for Eleanor had been an old man's folly and meant nothing, that without Molly he, like Fenn, would lose his identity and reason. But Eleanor Masefield was dead and Molly would never be sure if George's expression of love for his wife would have been so certain if the woman had lived.

George never found out how the local police came to have keys to Frank Oliver's house. Perhaps Oliver had given some to a neighbour.

The house was at the end of the terrace, backing on to a canal. At the end of the road was a series of railway arches and every twenty minutes a train would go past at chimney-pot height, rattling the windows and making the light shades shudder. In the house next door a fat old lady in an upstairs window stared down at them. The window was dirty and George could see nothing of the room but it seemed to him that the woman was laughing at them.

George was not sure whether he would be invited into the house. Oliver had stopped keeping birds of prey there some years before, so the excuse that he was a Wild Life Act Inspector no longer applied. When Pritchard pulled up behind the police car already parked close to the kerb, George stayed in his seat and made no move to accompany the superintendent.

'Come on,' Pritchard said. 'What are you waiting for?'

'I thought I might be in the way,' George said.

'No,' Pritchard said. He nodded at the uniformed policeman who waited impassively on the pavement. 'I'll tell them you're a civilian expert. That's true, isn't it? There might be all sorts of papers which would mean nothing to me. We might be breaking a few rules, but it'll save a lot of time in the end. See?' He grinned.

'I didn't help much at Puddleworth. All Fenn's paperwork was immaculate. It was possible to trace all his British birds of prey back to captive breeding pairs.'

'Ah well,' Pritchard said. 'I think we'll find things are a bit different here.'

He ambled up to one of the constables, his big face puckered into a smile, and clapped him on the shoulder.

'Good of you to come, lads,' he bellowed. 'Good of you to help us out. Well then, are you going to let us in? I expect you're busy. We country chaps don't know the sort of problems you face. You've got a terrible crime rate, I hear.'

Bemused, they opened the door for him. When he and George were inside he closed the door firmly behind him so the policemen were left outside on the pavement.

'Don't worry, lads!' he said as he shut the door. 'I'll drop the keys in at the station.'

They were standing in a dark, windowless hall. There was lino, patterned like wood block, on the floor, and stairs with brown carpet directly ahead of them. The house seemed dusty and airless but not dirty. Oliver, after all, had known that he would be away for a few days. He had been in Sarne for at least three days before the murder if Eleanor's story about the blue van was to be believed.

'Where was Oliver staying in Sarne?' George asked suddenly as Pritchard let him into the small sitting room. 'Do you know?'

Pritchard shook his head. 'We're not sure,' he said, 'but there was space enough for him to sleep in the van. Unless his wife put him up and isn't telling.'

'You don't know where the van was parked?'

'Not on the council estate where the Olivers live, but he's too clever to do that anyway. We should have more news when we get back – the lads are working on that today. There wasn't a sleeping bag in the van, or any clothes, but if he's camping out now, lying low, he would have taken those with him.'

'I'm sorry,' George said. 'Perhaps I shouldn't have asked. It was none of my business.'

'I'll tell you,' Pritchard said, 'if you're poking your nose where it's not wanted. Now then, let's have a look in here.'

After the darkness of the hall the room seemed suddenly light, but it was so cluttered that the impression was soon lost. George thought that Oliver's family could have taken no furniture with them when they went. Against one wall stood a table and dining chairs which looked as if they had been produced during the austerity of war. There was a settee and easy chair in mustard leatherette near to the gas fire and a large colour television set in one corner. On the wall furthest from the window was a unit of shelving and cupboards.

'If he was nicking birds, then selling them, he must have kept some record,' Pritchard said. He nodded towards the cupboards under the shelves which still held momentos of family life – souvenirs from Aberystwyth and Aberdeen, a photograph of thin children playing on a beach. 'We'll have a quick look round,' he said. 'Then we'll make a start in there.'

He led George through a glass door into the kitchen. Standing in the middle of the room he could have touched the walls on either side of him. The white distemper on the walls was peeling and there were flakes of it on the painted floor. The sink was old, made of white enamel. There was a long cupboard with a few tins of food, a box of tea bags, some powdered milk, and next to it an ancient gas stove and a refrigerator. Everything was reasonably clean and tidy but it was obvious that Oliver had not cared about the house. No rooms had been decorated, no new carpet or furniture had been bought, since Nan had left. The only unusual feature in the kitchen was a large chest freezer which took up the whole of one wall. The freezer was not switched on and when Pritchard lifted the lid it was empty.

'What would he want that for then?' Pritchard asked. 'I suppose it was useful with a big family and he didn't bother to get rid of it.'

'No,' George said. 'I don't think it was that. When he had his own birds here he would have kept their food in it.'

Pritchard looked surprised.

'Raptors eat animals,' George said. 'Rabbits, mice, day-old chicks. It's much easier to buy them in bulk and keep them frozen.'

Pritchard raised his eyebrows. 'I always thought falconry was a romantic sort of hobby,' he said. 'I saw that film – Kes – years ago and thought it was great. I didn't expect a freezer full of corpses.'

From the kitchen there was a back door into the garden. Pritchard had a key but the door was stiff as if it was seldom used. After transferring his birds Oliver would have had no reason to go out there. The aviaries still stood but they were rusting and full of rubbish and the grass and weeds were waist high. The place smelled of cats and the stagnant canal beyond the wire-mesh cages. There were signs of the garden that had been there before. Straggly flowers bloomed among the weeds and in one corner an enormous crown of rhubarb, its leaves the size of elephant ears, still survived.

Upstairs there was nothing of interest. There were three bedrooms and a bathroom with a huge white bath stained by a dripping tap. Oliver still used the middle room which he must have shared with his wife. The bed was made and there were clothes in the chest of drawers. The largest bedroom still contained two sets of bunks for the boys and the walls and curtains were covered in brightly coloured aeroplanes. The smallest, where the girls must have slept, had two single beds, so close to each other that they almost touched. George wondered if Oliver had put up the wallpaper for his sons, if he had participated at all in the life of the family. Perhaps it had all been left to Mrs Oliver and his only role had been to give her more children. Yet the trinkets from Wales and Scotland, the photographs of the beach, showed that in the beginning at least there had been family holidays. They must have had something in common then. George found the house depressing and wished they could leave. Pritchard however, back in Oliver's room, seemed unmoved.

'We'll leave all this to the experts,' he said, dismissively waving his hand over the double bed with the nylon sheets, the candlewick bedspread. 'I'll let them in this afternoon and they can search it properly then. Let's see what we can find in the downstairs cupboards.'

He bounded down the stairs like a big friendly dog in search of a chocolate treat.

At first the contents of the cupboards were disappointing. The first contained a jumble of papers as if letters, paid bills, magazines were put in there only because Oliver was afraid to throw them away. Pritchard sifted through the receipts, the forms explaining how to fill out other forms, with a thorough and delicate attention which impressed George. He seemed convinced that somewhere amid the debris they would find a clue to Oliver's whereabouts.

The next cupboard was more fruitful. It was almost empty and the contents were ordered as if Oliver needed to keep it tidy. The first find was a card index system in a small box which lised raptor species in alphabetical order. Each card was hand written and had obviously been amended and updated. Pritchard handed it to George.

'Is this anything to do with the work at Puddleworth?' he asked.

George took the box and began to look carefully at the cards.

'No,' he said. 'It's nothing to do with Puddleworth. It's a list of the breeding sites of most of the rarer raptors in Britain.' He pulled card after card from the box. 'There isn't only information of falcons and hawks,' he said. 'There's a whole section on owls, and here's a card on buzzard and one on golden eagle.' He read the eagle card in detail. 'That's astonishing,' he said. 'He's got a record of an amazing number of Scottish breeding sites.'

'Is it important?' Pritchard asked.

'It means that Oliver had access to incredibly detailed information. He must have had contacts all over the country telling him exactly where birds were breeding. There's no proof of course that he was stealing birds' eggs or young from these sites. He might have been selling the information to other dishonest falconers or egg collectors. But I can't think of any legitimate reason for keeping it like this. Look – there are even Ordnance Survey map grid references. If he were just an interested birdwatcher he wouldn't need that sort of detail.'

'But it doesn't help us find Oliver?'

'No,' George said. 'I don't suppose it does.'

Underneath the card index box were a couple of files containing documents relating to Oliver's birds at Puddleworth – registration forms, and a letter from the Department of the Environment notifying him of a Wildlife Act Inspector's visit. Then there was a large, flat cardboard box which might once have contained a shirt. On the top in large, childish handwriting Oliver had written 'correspondence'. Inside, there were just two sheets of paper. One, a flimsy carbon copy of a typewritten sheet, read like a shopping list, starting with six buzzard and ending with peregrine. It commented that demand for peregrine this year was limited but added that it was essential to obtain the Sarne birds for an influential overseas buyer.

'I understand this,' Pritchard said. 'It's a list of the birds and eggs Oliver has been asked to take. It shows he was working for a lot of different buyers.'

'Yes,' George said, 'but I don't think Oliver can have compiled it. Even if he had access to a typewriter at Puddleworth I don't imagine that his typing would be as good as this. And why just keep a carbon copy if he were making the list for his own use? I think Oliver was employed as an agent by someone who sent him this list and paid him once the birds were delivered.'

'We can check to see if it was typed at Puddleworth,' Pritchard said. 'We might still find that Fenn is involved after all.'

He handed George the second sheet of paper in the box. 'What do you make of this?'

It was a piece of lined A4 like a sheet from a student's refill pad. It was ruled into three columns with the widest column in the middle and it was in Oliver's handwriting. It was obviously Oliver's response to the shopping list. It was a detailed plan of campaign. He had decided when each species should be taken and which site it should be taken from. It was set out in chronological order and in the first column was a series of dates running from the beginning of March to the second week of July. In the middle column, next to each date were the bird's common and scientific names, followed by the exact site of the nest and notes of any wardening schemes or electronic protection. In the last column was one of two initials – either FLO or TW.

George scanned quickly down the list, handed the paper to Pritchard and pointed to the reading for 23 May. 'Peregrine,' Pritchard read. 'Falco Peregrinus. Sarne. Eyrie on rock face above hill path. Rope needed. No danger of disturbance. FLO.' He looked at George, 'He was wrong about there being no danger of disturbance, wasn't he? But at least we know it was him.'

'We might know that he stole the peregrines,' George said. 'We don't know, do we, that he murdered Eleanor Masefield?'

'We've got bloody good circumstantial evidence,' Pritchard boomed. 'We found her shoe on the hill, the birds were missing, the body's dumped near the birds where Oliver was working. All we need to do now is find the bugger and get a confession.'

'I wonder,' George said quietly, 'who TW is. FLO is obviously Frank Oliver, but TW appears on the list more often than he does. If we could find him he might lead us to Oliver.'

'You're brilliant,' Pritchard said. 'Of course.'

'TW is on the list to rob a merlin nest tomorrow,' George said. 'On Farthing Ridge.'

Pritchard slapped George on the back. 'I think,' he said, 'you and I had better go bird watching.'

Chapter Six

Molly spent all that day at Sarne. For the first time since Eleanor's death she felt an itch of resentment. George had not asked her to go with him to Puddleworth, nor asked if she would mind being left in the depressing house for another day.

Of course we take each other for granted, she thought. We've been married for more than thirty years. Yet she still resented his escape from Gorse Hill. Because he felt in some way responsible for Eleanor's death, George had become involved in the search for her murderer, but he had left *her* in Gorse Hill with its bereaved and unhappy occupants to go on a jaunt to a Falconry Centre in Shropshire. It seemed unfair. He had pushed her tolerance too far.

She went downstairs not knowing quite what to expect, but everything seemed much as usual. In the dining room her table had been laid for breakfast and in the hall Helen and Fanny were on their way out to walk to the high school. Their school uniform was black and the girls looked tired, drained of all colour. A girl brought her coffee and poached eggs and she ate alone in one corner of the big room. She was just finishing the meal when Richard Mead came in. Molly did not know what to make of him. On previous visits she had thought him competent, that he held the family business together and took all the important decisions. He had allowed Eleanor to be the figurehead but had managed perfectly well without her interference.

It was a surprise then that without Eleanor he seemed weak and rather foolish. Now he seemed to want someone to talk to. He had given Nan Oliver some time off, he said. It must be a terrible time for her too. Would Molly mind finding lunch for herself in

Sarne? Molly said that of course she wouldn't mind, but still he would not leave her to her coffee and morning paper. She suggested in the end that he find another cup and share the coffee with her. He seemed inordinately grateful for the invitation as if he would never have had the confidence to suggest it himself.

'I don't know what to do,' he said, staring at her helplessly. 'There are more guests booked in next Saturday. Should I tell them we've had to cancel?'

'Surely that depends what you and Veronica want to do with Gorse Hill,' Molly said. 'Do you want to stay and run it as an hotel?'

'Oh yes,' he said. 'I should think so.'

'How is Veronica this morning?'

'She was still asleep when I last looked,' he said. 'But I suppose she'll be waking soon.'

He hesitated and Molly could tell that he wanted something from her. In her mood of resentment she found something irritating in the demands he made of her. She had been a social worker for long enough. That phase of her life was over. But the expression on his long face was so pathetic that she could not get up and walk away.

'Is there anything I could do to help?' she asked. Again he was childishly grateful, and her irritation returned.

'Would you go up to Veronica?' he said, all in a rush. 'Last night I only seemed to upset her. I don't think she even understood exactly what happened. She'll be calmer with you. Explain to her about Eleanor's death. I can't bear to see her crying.'

'Are you sure,' Molly asked, 'that she wouldn't prefer to see you when she wakes?'

'Yes,' he said. 'This way will be much better.'

She suspected that he only wanted to save himself unpleasantness. Now it was obvious that Veronica needed more than cups of tea and buttered toast, he was too weak to support his wife through her grief. She followed him up the stairs to Veronica's room and tapped on the door. Inside there was the sound of a woman stirring, a faint, muffled response. Richard Mead fled.

Molly pushed open the door. The room was large but there was little light. Flounced curtain made of pale pink velvet were still drawn to shut out the sunshine. Molly approached the bed awkwardly.

'I'm sorry to disturb you,' she said. 'Richard asked me to see you. May I open the curtains a little?'

She felt the conversation would be easier if she could see the woman's face. There was another sound from the bed which she took to be agreement so she went to the window and pulled a plaited cord which drew the curtains apart. The room, Molly thought, was decorated according to Veronica's taste. She found it hard to imagine Richard Mead there. The room was predominantly pink. There were white fitted wardrobes with gold handles, but the wallpaper had a small rose print and the carpet was the colour of strawberry water ice. The sheets had roses on to match the wallpaper. They were crumpled and the shiny pink cover had slipped to the floor. Veronica was frowning as if she were struggling to consciousness from a deep sleep. She propped herself on to one elbow. Despite her ordeal she looked healthy and rested, as if even in this her innocence had protected her.

'Is it true?' she asked. 'Mother is dead?'

Molly nodded. Veronica lay-back on her pillow.

'I thought it might have been a dream,' she said. 'A nightmare. I slept so deeply.'

'The doctor gave you something to knock you out,' Molly said.

'I made a fool of myself,' Veronica said. 'Mother would have been angry.' She turned her head to look at Molly. 'Why are you here?' she asked simply.

'Richard asked me to come to see you to explain what had happened. He was afraid he might upset you again.'

'I see,' Veronica said. 'Of course. He wouldn't want to see me upset.'

'Do you remember what happened to your mother?' Molly said. 'Or would you like me to tell you as much as we know? The police will probably be here to ask some questions later.'

Veronica looked closely at Molly but ignored the question.

'Richard *is* all right?' she said. 'He's not angry with me for being so silly?'

'Of course not. He's just worried about you.'

'He doesn't like unpleasantness,' Veronica said. 'That's why he would never stand up to Mother.' She sat up in the bed, leaning against the padded bedhead. Molly watched her snatch a glimpse of herself in a mirror on the wall opposite and pat a curl into place. It was an habitual gesture of comfort and probably meant nothing, but Molly could not help being shocked.

'Tell me what happened,' Veronica said, unaware of Molly's reaction. 'I don't remember very clearly.'

'Your mother's body was found in the birds of prey's weathering ground,' Molly said uncomfortably. 'The birds hadn't killed her. The police think she was murdered on the hill. One of her shoes was found there.'

'What was she doing on the hill?'

'The peregrine chicks were stolen.'

'So she was right,' Veronica said. She was astounded, shocked from the lethargy of her drugged sleep. 'She wasn't mad at all.'

'No,' Molly said. 'I never thought she was mad.'

'Do the police think she was killed by someone who was taking the peregrines?'

That seemed to matter to her. Molly could imagine that it would be easier for her to accept her mother's death if there were some, reason for it. A random, motiveless murder must seem the worst kind of injustice.

'Yes,' Molly said carefully. 'I suppose she must have surprised the thieves while they were taking the young birds. She was killed by a heavy blow to the head.'

'Do the police know who killed her?' Veronica asked. Molly had never seen her so still or intense.

'They think they do. They're looking for Nan Oliver's ex-husband, Frank, and her son. Frank Oliver owned a blue van and he works for a falconer. He's disappeared.'

It seemed to Molly then that Veronica changed again. She became the woman Molly had known and could recognize, the silly, self-centred woman who could gossip for hours about the new curate's relationship with the cub scout leader.

'Poor Mrs Oliver,' she said, but Molly thought she was almost excited by the news that Frank Oliver was wanted for her mother's murder.

'So there *was* a blue van,' Veronica continued. 'I was never sure. I thought perhaps Mother was making the whole thing up to persuade the RSPB to warden the site. Or just to worry us.' She seemed to have forgotten her theory of her mother's insanity. 'I'm glad in a way that Mother was right. She usually was.'

Molly sensed some of the old bitterness. How would Veronica, vain and pretty and dependent, manage without her mother? She might enjoy the freedom at first as she had when she was first married, but Molly felt that the emptiness and depression of the previous day would return. The calm was as unnatural as the ritual glimpse in the mirror.

'I'll get up now,' Veronica said. She swung her legs out of the bed, pushed feet into fluffy slippers. 'I'll go to Richard. Thank you for coming to see me. It helped a lot.'

As she was expected to, Molly left the room. Only then did she realize that Veronica had not asked how her children had been affected by Eleanor's death. She was, Molly thought, very like a child herself.

Molly wandered downstairs. In the pleasant, sunny house, she felt trapped and uncomfortable, and her futile resentment of George returned. She had accepted his admiration of Eleanor Masefield and had agreed to come to Gorse Hill because she knew he had enjoyed Eleanor's company. Now she realized how much she had disliked Eleanor, and began to blame the woman, quite unreasonably, for her own discomfort. That's ridiculous, she thought. Eleanor Masefield was a victim, an innocent witness of a crime. She got in the way. But the notion that Eleanor had, in some way, contributed to her own death remained with her and did so for the rest of the investigation.

Molly decided to go for a walk. She could at least escape that far. It was a great pleasure to leave the house where she felt like an unwelcome and uninvited guest. The mild wind blew into her face. The sun came out in occasional bright bursts, setting fire to the huge banks of gorse. There was a wheatear on the short grass and a skylark was singing. She turned her back on the hill and walked down the lane towards the town. Away from the hill the landscape changed. On one side of the road was a field of sheep, with big, black-faced lambs and on the other a stretch of growing corn. The wind blew through the corn in a long, green wave, and brought back a memory so vivid and sharp that she had to stop walking.

We were married on a day like this, she thought, unaccountably excited. The wind smelled of salt and the sun was hotter but it felt just the same. They had been married quietly and quickly in Suffolk, where they were both based with the army just after the war. Neither had close relatives to invite, so they had invited no one at all, just two acquaintances to be witnesses. 'What has it to do with anyone else?' George had asked and she had agreed. After the simple ceremony they had cycled to the coast through fields of corn, riper than this one, through the wide and empty country. The wind blew over the fields from the sea and all the way along the straight, narrow road she longed to touch him, but they did not even link fingers and they hardly spoke. They spent one night in a small white cottage at Minsmere before George returned to Berlin.

I knew what he was like then, she thought. He was just the same: compulsive, frightened of failure. I loved him for it. I knew he would go back to Berlin because he had work to do, though he could have spent longer with me. We could have had a real honeymoon. In the same way he felt he had to go to Puddleworth with Alan Pritchard. He would give me the same sort of freedom.

She leaned over a wooden gate and looked down the valley towards the town. The wind blew through a small group of trees, turning the undersides of the leaves to the sun, making them silver grey with reflected light. It had been a long time since she had thought of George with that degree of intensity. They seemed too old and too used to each other for introspection.

Perhaps I should leave that to the teenagers, she thought, and remembered Helen and the Oliver boy. She hoped they would be happy.

Her resentment gone, she considered again the events of the morning. Away from Gorse Hill the reluctance of Richard to talk to his wife seemed curious, even sinister. The death of Eleanor Masefield seemed to have reversed the relationship between husband and wife. Veronica, even in her grief and confusion, was stronger and more decisive and Richard had gone to pieces. The girls had been left alone to cope with their shock and grief as best they could. Molly was intrigued by the family, and the possibility of a prolonged stay at Gorse Hill was no longer a hardship. She wanted to find out more about them. She wanted to know what was going on.

Perhaps I'll find out who killed Eleanor Masefield before George does, she thought, elated by the wind and the memory of her passion for him. The idea was a challenge and an amusement. It would teach George, she thought, to take her for granted. She pulled her jacket around her and walked into the town.

Helen saw Molly in the town, but turned down an empty side street so that the woman should not see her. She did not want anyone to know that she had left school early. She had only gone into school to see Laurie. Her father had said that she and Fanny could stay at home and he seemed so fraught and distressed about Mother that she had felt she should have stayed at Gorse Hill to look after him. But she had needed to talk to Laurie, to find out why he had disappeared from Gorse Hill the day before, to be reassured that he had nothing to do with her grandmother's death. So she had walked to the school on the other side of the town, as usual but when she got there no one had seen Laurie and she had left again during the mid-morning break.

In the town most of the people she passed were elderly. The small shops catered for their needs – there was a preponderance of chemists and shops selling Crimplene dresses, surgical stockings and winceyette nightdresses. The young mothers who still lived in

Sarne went to the superstore on the bypass for their groceries and to Hereford for their clothes. Sarne itself seemed intent on preserving the serious nature of shopping and would have preferred ration books and Eastern European queues. There was no sense of fun or pleasure, no wine bars, boutiques or bookshops. On other occasions Helen would have been irritated by the tedium of the place but today she welcomed it and walked on without speaking to anyone.

She knew where Laurie lived though she had never been to his home. She had visited the council estate occasionally with her mother, delivering commodes and walking frames to elderly residents for the WRVS. She had never been there alone and as she walked past the pretty, well-kept gardens she felt that people were peering behind lace curtains and that everyone knew who she was and why she was there. Outside the Llewellyns' house two toddlers with runny noses stopped playing in the jungle of long grass, pushed their faces against the bars of the broken gate and stared at her as she walked past.

The house on the end, where Laurie lived, was a little larger than the others and although the garden was tidier than the Llewellyns' it did not meet the general standard. The grass had been roughly cut but there were no flowers in the front border and the hedge was overgrown. As she walked up the path to the front door Helen realized that she was shaking.

Nan Oliver opened the door. She had been awake all night. Michael and Carol had been reluctant to go back to sleep after being wakened by the police and even when they had settled she had been too worried to sleep. There had been no news of Steve.

'Hello, Mrs Oliver,' Helen said. It would have been so much easier if Laurie's mother had not been there. 'Is Laurie at home?'

'Why?' Nan Oliver demanded. What did this patronizing madam from Gorse Hill want from her family? Nan had always kept her private life separate from her work. 'We had nothing to do with Mrs Masefield's death.' Helen was bewildered. She had not expected such hostility.

'Of course not,' she said. 'Laurie's a friend. I'd like to talk to him.'

'You'd better come in,' Nan Oliver said. 'He's upstairs. I'll give him a shout.'

She showed Helen into the front room. 'It's a mess,' she said. 'The police were here until all hours last night.'

'I'm sorry,' Helen said, as if she were in some way responsible for the inconvenience caused by the police.

On her way out of the room to call Laurie, Mrs Oliver hesitated.

'I'm sorry,' she said formally, 'about your grandmother's death. It must have been a terrible shock, especially to your mother.'

'Yes,' Helen said. She was grateful for the expected proprieties. 'It was.'

Then the woman was gone. Helen could hear her heavy, tired footsteps on the stairs. She returned a few minutes later followed by Laurie, and stood just inside the door.

'Would you like some tea?' she said immediately, so that Helen could not look at Laurie at once to see how he seemed, but had to say politely that she would like tea, thank you, and that she took milk but not sugar and no, she didn't mind it strong.

Mrs Oliver gave them a piercing and perceptive stare, then went into the kitchen and they could hear the sound of running water and the banging of crockery.

'She doesn't like me,' Helen whispered. It seemed more important then than her grandmother's death.

Laurie smiled. 'She doesn't like any of our girlfriends,' he said. He looked tired, like his mother, with black smudges under his eyes.

'Where did you go?' she cried suddenly. 'Yesterday. I looked for you and you weren't there.'

'I'm sorry,' he said. 'I didn't know. About your grandmother. I had a row with my father. Then I came home.'

'But you should have told me,' she said. She would never have treated him like that.

'I'm sorry,' he said again and he began to cry. She moved next to him, put her arms round him and pulled his head on to her shoulder, then stroked his stiff, black hair.

'It's all right,' she said, as if talking to a baby, 'I didn't realize. I thought you didn't care any more. I thought you had just forgotten about me.'

He pulled away from her indignantly. It seemed inconceivable to him now that he could have just forgotten about her, though that was precisely what had happened. He convinced himself and her that she mattered more to him than anything. There were still tears in his eyes.

'No,' he said. 'Of course not. I was so upset after seeing my father I didn't want you to see me like that. I didn't think you could care for someone so weak.'

'Silly,' she said. 'You should have known. I don't think you're weak.' She paused and took his hand. 'Even if you were,' she said, 'I'm strong enough for both of us.' They sat for a moment in silence. She looked towards the kitchen. 'Can we go for a walk later?' she said. 'I want to talk.'

Before he could answer his mother came in. He was grateful for the interruption. He was in no state to make any decision. He was happy to be sitting there next to Helen. Helen thought Nan Oliver must have been listening but she looked at the older woman with increased confidence. Nan Oliver stared back. She had too much to cope with, she thought, without Helen Mead upsetting Laurie. She saw his tears and despite, her exhaustion felt protective and anxious. Laurie seemed oblivious of the tension between Helen and his mother. He had been learning a new song and the melody eddied round his mind. He could concentrate on nothing else. It had been a way of escaping the worry about his father and Steve and now it had taken him over.

'Shall we go for a walk?' Helen asked, setting her cup and saucer on a small table. 'You look as if you could do with some air.'

'His dinner's nearly ready,' Nan Oliver said quickly. 'He should stay here in case there's any news.'

Laurie hovered between them, his mind filled with music.

'I'm not really hungry,' he said. He did not want to offend Helen again so soon. His mother would get over it. It did not occur to him that she really needed his company. She had always been so strong.

Nan Oliver shrugged her shoulders, tired and beaten.

'Don't be long,' she said, with a last flicker of resistance. 'You'll have to be here when the little ones get home from school in case I have to go out.'

On the doorstep he hesitated, realizing for the first time how he was abandoning her, but Helen had taken his hand and was pulling him down the path.

Now they were out of the house Helen was not quite sure where to go. They wandered back towards the town.

'Do you think your father killed Eleanor?' Helen asked. It would be rather brave, she thought, to be the girlfriend of a murderer's son.

'I don't know,' he mumbled, still affected by the music and the reproach in his mother's face.

'It must be a dreadful worry,' she said, sympathetic, understanding.

'I'm not bothered about Dad,' he said. 'I don't feel he belongs to us any more. It's Steve. I wish I knew where he was.'

'Perhaps he's hiding,' she said. 'Not because he was involved at all but because he's heard the police are looking for your father and he's frightened. You must know him well. Where would he go? Friends?'

Laurie shook his head. 'The police have tried them,' he said.

'Didn't he have any special places where he might be hiding?' she asked, determined to help. 'There was an old pigsty at the bottom of the garden at Gorse Hill where I used to go when I was a kid. I liked sitting there, especially when it was raining. Then I seemed cut off from the world. If I were running away that's where I'd go.'

Laurie shook his head. 'By the time we moved here we were too old for that sort of thing,' he said, so that she felt foolish.

By that time they had reached the empty market square at the centre of the town. There was the smell of seed and grain from the agricultural suppliers on the corner and of frying bacon from the café on the end of the high street. The wind blew scraps of straw in swirls.

'I'm hungry,' she said. 'Shall we go in and have a coffee?'

He drifted after her, trying to think of an excuse to go home to his mother. The café was run by a fat bald man with a cigarette in his mouth. Helen had never been in there before. There was a full-length window looking on to the street, so they sat at the table like dummies in a shop window, fully visible from the pavement.

'Oh no,' Helen said. 'There's that little lady who's staying at Gorse Hill, I hope she doesn't tell Dad that I've missed school.'

Laurie said nothing. He wished he were back at home in his bedroom, with his guitar. His passion for Helen had faded. She was just another woman who might look after him and who made demands on him.

'Perhaps she can help us to find your brother,' Helen said, suddenly excited. She was determined to make herself indispensable to Laurie's family. Then they would have to like her. 'Her husband's a private detective. He's the man Eleanor called in to look after the peregrines.'

Laurie muttered that in that case he could not be a very good detective but Helen was already on her feet, and to Laurie's embarrassment began to wave.

Molly bought a mug of coffee and joined them at the table. She said nothing and waited for them to speak.

'Laurie's worried about his brother,' Helen said. Now that the woman was sitting beside her she seemed more intelligent, more daunting than Helen had previously realized. The girl was suddenly shy. She did not want to make a fool of herself even for Laurie. 'We wondered if you had any ideas about how we should start looking for him.'

'The police are very good at that sort of thing,' Molly said. She was thinking that this might be an opportunity to prove to George that their business and their marriage were an equal partnership, that she was as skilled at gaining information as he was. She drank some of the milky coffee and looked at Laurie.

'Did Steve tell you where he had met his father to discuss the proposed new job?' she asked.

He thought back to the angry confrontation in his bedroom.

'They met in a pub,' he said. 'In the Hop Pole.'

That, thought Molly, was an extraordinary stroke of luck. She had known the landladies of the Hop Pole for years.

'I could ask in there for you,' Molly said. 'One of the regular customers may have overheard their discussion. They might have heard Steve and your father making plans.'

'Shall we come with you?' Helen asked. Molly shook her head.

'You're well known,' she said. 'There's been a lot of publicity about the murder. I could be more discreet. I'll tell you tonight if I have any luck.'

They left the café together. Molly, said goodbye and hurried off. Helen and Laurie stood awkwardly on the pavement.

'You don't mind me asking her?' Helen said.

'No, of course not. Why should I?'

'I don't suppose she'll be a lot of help.'

'Look,' he said suddenly. 'I've got to go back to be with Mum. All this has been terrible for her. I shouldn't have left her on her own.'

'Shall I come with you?' she asked.

'No,' he said. 'Better not.'

'I'll come to see you' she said. 'At home tomorrow. I won't go to school.'

He nodded agreement. She held him tight and turned her face to kiss him. He brushed his lips against hers then walked off, his head bent, his eyes on the pavement.

The Hop Pole was squashed into a side street off the high street. It had not been painted for years. The whitewash was stained and green and the windows so dirty that artificial light was needed inside all day. The sign had fallen down in a gale and no one had been employed to replace it. The pub was run by two elderly spinster sisters, the Cadwalladers, and had previously been owned by their father. It had been George's local when he was a young man – he could remember the Cadwalladers as stylish young ladies. Now he said it typified the town and would not stay in Sarne without visiting it.

The younger sister, Mary, was in her late sixties and was known to her regulars by her Christian name. She was pleasing, eccentric and not very clever. The elder, Gertrude, was Miss Cadwallader to all her customers, even her contemporaries. Miss Cadwallader was mean, efficient and ruthless. She was the sole figure of authority in the Hop Pole and was intimidated neither by unruly customers nor the licensing laws. The pub stayed open for as long as she was still making money. She had tremendous stamina, and could drink most of the men in the place under the table. She liked what she called 'a certain class of gentleman' in the Hop Pole and counted among her regulars a doctor who had been convicted of drunk driving and retired early, several teachers and the clerk to the parish council. All her regulars drank in the public bar. The lounge was cold and dusty. It was reserved for strangers to the town and for the under-age drinkers of whom she disapproved, but whose money she had not the heart to turn away. If some newcomer, unknowing, wandered into the public bar and took one of the best seats near to the fire she would tap sharply on the bar.

'Excuse me young man,' she would say, irrespective of the intruder's age. 'That's Mr Gregory's chair. He'll be in shortly. I think you might be more comfortable here.'

She would direct him to a stool near to the bar and question him about his status, his family, his occupation. If he turned out to be a sales representative she would suggest that in the future he might prefer to use the lounge which was usually quieter.

The question of what Miss Cadwallader did with all her money was a matter of great speculation in the Hop Pole. Occasionally she allowed Mary to buy herself a new dress or to go on a coach trip to see the Dutch bulb fields or the Austrian Alps, but she spent nothing on herself.

When Molly went into the pub it was half past two. A group of old men were playing dominoes in a corner and Mary was alone behind the bar. She looked, Molly thought, uncannily like the Queen Mother. She had wispy hair, flowery clothes and a permanent, bemused smile.

'Molly!' she said. 'Is it really you? What a lovely surprise. I must call Gertrude.'

'Don't disturb Miss Cadwallader yet,' Molly said. Mary was a better gossip than her sister. She chattered without realizing the implication of what she was saying. Gertrude was too discreet. She saw herself in a privileged position, like a doctor or a priest, and might be unwilling to pass on any information gained behind the bar. 'Have a drink with me first.'

Delighted by this attention Mary said she would have a sweet sherry. She poured a glass of beer for Molly.

'How's George?' Mary asked. 'It's so long since he's been here. We do miss him.'

'He's busy,' Molly said, then lowered her voice melodramatically. Mary loved excitement. 'We've been staying at Gorse Hill. He's helping the police!'

That sent Mary into a nervous fluster of pleasure. 'How terrible!' she said. Poor dear Mrs Masefield. How she would be missed. 'Is it true,' she whispered, 'that the police are looking for Nan Oliver's husband?'

'I think they are,' Molly said. 'And her son Stephen. The police haven't been here to talk to you then?'

'No,' Mary said. 'Why should they do that?' She leant across the bar, her eyes gleaming with curiosity.

'I understand,' Molly said, 'that Frank Oliver met Stephen in here one evening last week.'

'No,' Mary said. 'Really? Do you know which evening that was?'

'Last Thursday,' Molly said. 'Do you remember seeing them?'

'It was very quiet in here on Thursday,' Mary said. 'They would have been in the lounge of course. I usually serve in the lounge in the evening. I wonder what they were like.'

She was desperate to remember. She wanted the importance of being a witness.

'I know!' she said in triumph. 'They came in quite early in the evening and the bar was empty. Now I think of it the boy did have something of Nan Oliver about the eyes. The man was very dark, quite short. Would that be him?'

Molly nodded. 'I don't suppose,' she said, 'that you heard what they were saying.'

Mary began to polish glasses in a frenzy of concentration.

'I couldn't hear from the bar,' she said. 'They were talking very quietly. I wasn't curious about them, you see. I didn't recognize Stephen Oliver. But I did go over there to put some coal on the fire.'

She put down the cloth.

'They were talking about passports,' she said suddenly. 'The older man asked the boy if he had a passport. The boy said. "No of course not. I've never been anywhere." Then the older man said it didn't matter. He could get a British Visitor's passport at the post office. "I haven't got any money," the boy said. The man said not to worry about money. He would pay. He would get all his expenses back. I thought they were discussing a business trip abroad.' She looked pleased with herself and sipped the sherry. 'There,' she said. 'Do you think I should tell the police?'

Gertrude Cadwallader appeared suddenly behind her sister, seemed to tower over her. She was more solid than Mary, tall and broad with a heavy jaw and a big bust. Hop Pole legend had it that there had been many suitors for Mary but none for Gertrude and that Gertrude had frightened them all away through jealousy.

'Isn't it exciting,' Mary said nervously. 'Molly's been telling me about dear Eleanor Masefield's murder. The police are looking for Frank Oliver and he was here, last week, making plans.'

'It's never been my policy,' Miss Cadwallader said, 'to give any information to the police. We have our livelihood to consider. You must do as you think best, of course.'

She began to make polite regal conversation to Molly and ignored Mary's obvious disappointment. There was no doubt that Mary would do as her sister wished.

'Well perhaps it would be best to give the information to George,' Mary said brightly, interrupting them as if she had changed her mind of her own accord. 'I don't suppose we want policemen in the bar. You will tell him, Molly?'

'Of course,' Molly said. What a shame it was! she thought. Mary would have liked being collected in a police car and being taken to the station to make a statement to a handsome young policeman.

'Then perhaps George will want to come to see me,' Mary continued, consoling herself, 'to ask me some questions.'

'I'm sure he will,' Molly said and went out into the street where the wind had increased and dark rainclouds had covered the sun.'

Although she had half expected George to have returned when she arrived at Gorse Hill it was deserted. She supposed that Richard had taken Veronica away from the oppressive memories of the house. She wondered if she should tell the local police about the conversation overheard in the Hop Pole, but it seemed unnecessary. George and Pritchard would surely be back from Puddleworth soon.

As Molly entered the house the telephone was ringing. She hesitated, thinking it might stop or that someone else might come to answer it, but the noise continued. The office door was open and she went in and picked up the receiver.

'Hello,' said a man's precise voice. He spoke clearly but had a slight foreign accent. 'Is that Gorse Hill? Kerry Fenn suggested that I contact you. It's a business matter.'

'I'm sorry,' Molly said. 'This is Gorse Hill but I'm only a guest. None of the family is here. Perhaps I could take a message.'

But the man had already rung off.

Molly went into the lounge. As she sat reading, big raindrops began to splatter against the window pane. Helen must have gone back to school for the afternoon because she and Fanny arrived home together, running up the drive, trying to avoid the worst of the rain. They burst into the hall, noisy and breathless, shedding books and coats and satchels, then went upstairs and the house was quiet again.

George phoned late that afternoon. He would not be home, he said, for another day. They had discovered a useful lead at Oliver's home and Pritchard needed his help. He was apologetic but did not expect Molly to object. She said that was all right. She would find plenty to occupy her at Gorse Hill. It seemed to her still that this obsession with leads and chasing round the country was male dramatic nonsense. The answer to Eleanor's death lay in Sarne and she would find it before he did. Then she told him about the overheard conversation in the Hop Pole and she could tell he was impressed. That will teach him, she thought again, to take me for granted. She did not tell him about the phone call from the foreigner. It seemed to have no importance.

Chapter Seven

George and Pritchard arrived at Farthing Ridge at dusk. It was the highest hill in Shropshire, a long thin rib across the countryside. They had decided that the theft of the merlin eggs might take place at dawn the following day, so to be sure of catching the man Oliver had called TW they would have to stay there all night. The merlin had nested in a hawthorn tree close to an education authority field centre, high up in the hills. There was a track to the field centre and they could have driven there but the car would have given them away. They were worried too that TW might already be on the hill, keeping a watch on the track. So they had left the car at Farthingford, a hamlet with a line of farmworkers' grey cottages, an impressive grey chapel and a tiny school to serve the outlying farms. It was a longer walk than they had expected through bog and wet sheep-cropped grass. Pritchard soon lost his schoolboy enthusiasm for the chase and thought of Bethan and their large soft bed.

The wind had increased all day and in the evening had blown a band of cloud in from the Welsh mountains, so that when they arrived it was too dark to see more than the square shape of the field centre and the line of the hill beyond. Pritchard had been given permission to use the field centre, and a key, but it had not been equipped again for summer use and they knew it would be empty. The RSPB's roving warden was already there. He had not had access to the building and sat on the grass, leaning against one wall, sheltered from the wind. He was asleep.

George had contacted the RSPB although at first Pritchard had wanted no one to know that they wanted to go to the Farthing Ridge site.

'We'll have to tell them,' George had said. 'They might even have a warden there or volunteers keeping an eye on the site. If two strangers turn up they'll call out the local police and we'd look rather foolish then. They're used to keeping secrets.'

So he had telephoned an old friend who was Regional Officer for the society in the West Midlands.

'Do merlins breed on Farthing Ridge?' he asked. He gave the Ordnance Survey grid reference number found in Oliver's house.

The Regional Officer was astonished, suspicious, a little angry.

'How do you know that?' he asked. 'It's miles from anywhere. We hadn't any records of merlin in that area until a couple of our contract workers doing an uplands survey found the nest earlier in the spring.'

George ignored the question.

'Is it wardened?' he asked.

The man hesitated. 'No,' he said. 'We didn't think it was necessary.'

'I've information that someone wants to take the eggs,' George said. 'Tomorrow. The circumstances are a bit unusual. The suspected thief is wanted by the police on another, more serious matter. The police will be waiting at the site to get him. I thought I'd better let you know.'

'We ought to be involved,' the man said.

'I don't think the police will agree to that.'

'All the same. We need all the prosecutions we can get. Besides you might not find the nest by yourselves. It's not that easy, not in poor light. I'll send a lad to help you. He's been there several times during the season to see what's going on.'

Pritchard could hardly object to that, George thought, and said they would meet the roving warden there. The Regional Officer was about to hang up when George asked: 'Do the initials TW mean anything to you? I suppose they might belong to a falconer, but I can't think of anyone.'

'Theo Williams,' the man said. 'He's not a falconer. He's a taxidermist. He owns a very swanky business on the green at

Puddleworth and seems quite respectable. He works for some of the best museums. He specializes in preparing birds of prey for wealthy overseas falconers but he'll tackle anything from an elephant to a budgie if he's paid enough.'

'Is he legitimate?'

'No,' the man said. 'He's bent as hell, but he's too clever for us ever to have caught him. He's considered a great local naturalist in the area – he has a regular spot on the local radio – and he takes the opportunity to criticize the RSPB whenever he can. He seems to be running a personal vendetta against the society. He pretends to be a great supporter of birds for the people and encourages people to make nest sites of rare birds public. He says the RSPB is an elitist group, saving information for its own use. I think he's got his own motives for wanting information on rare breeding birds. Time and again birds disappear from nests where he's been seen. We just haven't been clever enough to catch him.'

'Well,' George said. 'Perhaps we'll get him tomorrow.'

'Good luck, George,' the Regional Officer said. 'I hope that you do.'

George thought that Pritchard might abandon the trip to the merlin site on Farthing Ridge once the identity of TW was known, but the policeman seemed to relish the excitement and discomfort of it. He did send some men to Williams' premises in Puddleworth, but the place was empty, and Pritchard decreed that the expedition should continue.

With boy scout resourcefulness he had procured sleeping bags, a Thermos flask and sandwiches. He had brought a powerful torch and when finally they arrived at the field centre he shone it towards the sleeping warden. The young man woke suddenly and quietly but sat still, his knees pulled in front of him, his head leaning back against the wall.

'Sorry,' he said. He had a flat north-country accent. 'I don't get much sleep this weekend. I was in mid-Wales. We've been very worried about red kites this year so we've been keeping a watch at the weekends.'

The Regional Officer had said that the warden's name was Lewis.

George never found out if that was his Christian or his surname. He was a pale, colourless man of indeterminate age, so intense and committed that George could not imagine him living in a real house with a real family. He seemed destined to spend his life sleeping under trees where red kites were nesting, sacrificing his youth to saving the country's wildlife. Pritchard must have recognized the exaggerated, almost religious, fervour too, because he treated him with a wary and respectful distance, as if he were a fanatical priest whose ideas he did not share.

Pritchard let them into the building. It had been unused all winter and was damp and cold. There was no electricity and no means of heating the place. A large window looked out on the hill, but by the time they arrived it was dark and starless and there was nothing to see. Pritchard put the sleeping bags on the concrete floor, so they had something soft to sit on, and Lewis described the site where the merlins were breeding.

'You can't see it from here,' he said. 'It's in a small dip in the hill. There are three hawthorn trees. They're stunted, but there's just enough shelter for them to grow. The merlins' nest is in the left-hand tree, it's an old crow's nest and would be a quick and easy climb. Williams'll have no trouble.'

'How would you expect Williams to get here?' Pritchard asked.

'By car up the track from the main road if he's feeling very sure of himself,' Lewis said. 'Otherwise he would leave the car in the village as we did, and walk.'

'Wouldn't he need to get the eggs into an incubator quickly?'

'There'd be no desperate hurry. He's probably got a portable incubator in his car.'

The boy was tired and cynical. Nothing the falconers would do could surprize and shock him. It was the older men with their years of experience in the law who seemed naïve and impressionable. Released from their desks they found it challenging to be sitting in the dark, waiting to catch the man who might lead them to Frank Oliver.

'Of course it doesn't do any good,' the boy said. 'All this cops and robbers stuff. That's why we've dropped a lot of our wardening schemes. We've found that the wardens only attract attention to the nests.'

He pulled a blanket around him and went back to sleep. George and Pritchard dozed but could not sleep. The floor was too uncomfortable. They were not used to sleeping under Welsh trees. Outside the wind blew and echoed around the moor.

George thought of Molly. She would enjoy this, he thought, but perhaps she's safer at Gorse Hill. He knew Pritchard had been impressed by the information about Stephen Oliver and the passport, but George, himself, had not been surprised. He knew that Molly, could magically persuade people to talk to her. He believed her capable of anything.

They saw the beam of Williams' car headlights before they heard the engine. The rumble of the car might have been the wind. Lewis was suddenly awake. As the light swung into the room through the window, the older men could see his eyes wide open, his head erect and alert. No one moved. The car stopped and the lights were switched off.

'He'll have to wait until there's a bit more light,' Lewis whispered. Inside the building there was no indication of dawn. Strangely broken by the gusts of wind, they could hear the rhythm of a voice speaking words they could not catch, then a faint line of music. Williams must be listening to his car radio. After about ten minutes the music stopped suddenly and the car door was opened, then slammed shut. There was the sound of footsteps on the road, then silence.

Pritchard jumped to his feet.

'Not yet!' Lewis said urgently. 'We want to do him for theft, not just for wilful disturbance. He has to get to the nest and take the eggs before he sees us.'

'Bugger that,' Pritchard said angrily. 'We want to question him about murder. I don't know what you're doing here anyway.'

Outside it was starting to get light. The wind had dropped and there was a persistent drizzle. The visibility was still very poor. The two men stared at each other, each refusing to give way.

'Just a few more minutes, Superintendent,' George murmured.

'He's not going to get away now. His car's here.' He turned to Lewis. 'If we wait outside,' he said, 'will Williams be able to see us from the nest site?'

The warden shook his head. 'I told you,' he said. 'There's a dip in the hill.'

They stood outside on the concrete track. Lewis pointed in the direction of the merlins' nest, but they could see nothing through the blanket of low cloud. Pritchard stood, peering through the greyness, waiting for Williams to return. The weather was worrying the warden and he said-suddenly: 'We'll go now. The eggs shouldn't be out of the nest in this. It's too cold. Better to do Williams for wilful disturbance than for the birds not to hatch.'

He led them off the road into the sodden grass. They climbed a drystone wall. Occasionally a sheep loomed out of the mist in front of them.

Then, so shocking that it might have been the sound of a gunshot, another car door slammed. They turned to see the shadow of a man running from the passenger side of Williams' expensive car down the concrete track towards the main road.

Pritchard was nearest to the track and had the best view of the man. 'Christ!' he shouted. 'It's Oliver. He was in the bloody car all the time.' He began to chase back towards the track and scrambled over the wall, swearing as he put his foot in a boggy puddle. The mud soaked his trousers and slowed him down. George knew that he would be no help. He was too old for that kind of run. He looked at Lewis. He was young and fit and would have had more chance of catching Oliver than Pritchard had. But he was concerned about his birds now. Oliver was none of his business and he had wanted to catch Williams for a long time. He walked on steadily up the hill towards the hawthorn trees.

'You stay by the car,' he said to George. 'If I frighten Williams he'll come back here. He won't go far. He's not daft. He won't go off on the moor on a day like this.'

George realized that what the boy said made sense and walked back towards the car, feeling that his age made him helpless and useless. There was nothing for him to do but wait. He supposed that the man in the car had been Oliver, but his eyesight was not as good as Pritchard's and he had seen only a blurred shape. This further illustration of his weakness irritated him more than his slowness. He would have liked to see the man they were chasing. Pritchard and Oliver had already disappeared into the low cloud at the end of the track, but it seemed to George in his mood of depression that Pritchard was unlikely to catch the man. Oliver was desperate, and though he was younger Pritchard was unfit and overweight.

The whole incident had become a farce. He supposed that Pritchard would arrange for roadblocks and extra police help, but that would take time. It had never occurred to them that Oliver might be accompanying Williams. It seemed easy in retrospect to feel foolish because they had not looked in the car before setting out on the hill, but Williams had been the target. They had not even any concrete proof that Oliver and Williams were acquaintances. George stood miserably by the car, while the rain dripped off the bottom of his Barbour jacket on to his trousers and into his boots.

Lewis and Williams returned to the car first. Lewis was furious.

'He's got rid of the eggs,' he said to George. 'I was too late. He'd been in the nest before I got there, but he must have heard me coming and dumped the eggs.' He turned to Williams. 'What did you do with them?' he demanded, his anger at last giving his face some colour. 'If I can find them now I might save them.'

The man shrugged and smiled. He did not look towards his car, did not mention that he'd had a passenger. 'I don't know what you're talking about,' he said. 'I don't know anything about eggs.'

George learned later that Williams had been the only son of a gamekeeper who worked on a big estate in southern Shropshire. He had been confused by his parents' conflicting attitudes to their employers. His mother had wanted her son to be like them, well-spoken, educated, cultured, but Theo had failed the 11-plus and her dreams of university and an academic career had come to nothing. His father had railed against the injustice of working for a man who knew next to nothing about his land, but pretended to know so much. He was an angry socialist who tried to explain to his son that there were only two classes in the country – the exploiters and the exploited, but made it clear that he despised the landowner for his unmasculine ways. He would not have wished to change places with him. So Williams had inherited envy and a bitterness at being excluded from his father and a softness and neshness from his mother. Occasionally his voice had an aggressive local accent. He wanted to belong to the area, but had travelled a lot and seemed to belong nowhere. Now he turned towards Lewis. 'If you've lost merlins' eggs, it's probably because of some natural predator,' he said. 'You're paranoid. Of course I've always said RSPB wardens cause a lot of birds to fail. They get too close to the nests and disturb the raptors.'

Lewis looked as though he would hit the man, but turned away.

'I'm going to look for those eggs,' he said to George. 'Don't wait for me. I'll make my own way back to Farthingford.'

As it got lighter the mist and low cloud seemed to lift a little, though the rain was just as heavy. George could see to the end of the track now, to the main road. A mail van drove past then disappeared into the cloud further up the ridge. George did not know what to do. If Williams decided that he wanted to drive away there was little he could do to stop him. He had no real official status. Williams, however, showed no immediate inclination to leave. Perhaps he wanted to know what they were doing there and how Oliver had come to disappear.

'Your friend ran away,' George said. He had grown tired of his role of passive, aged observer. He wanted to make something happen.

'What friend?' Williams said. He was a dark-haired, well-built man, dressed immaculately as if for the grouse moor.

'It was a foolish thing to do,' George continued. 'The police will catch him eventually.'

'I don't know what you're talking about,' Williams said uneasily. 'There was no one else in the car.' He thrust his hands in his pockets and stamped his feet up and down on the road as if he were cold. Unnerved, he restored to belligerence. 'Who are you anyway?'

The lie encouraged George. If Williams had had a legitimate passenger he would have said so. At least Pritchard had not disappeared on a fruitless chase. He felt strenthened by Williams' anxiety.

'My name's Palmer-Jones,' George said formally. 'I'm a Wildlife Act Inspector. I have reason to believe that in your car you have implements to assist you in the illegal removal of schedule one birds from the wild. I'd like to inspect the contents of your car.'

Williams looked at him in disbelief.

'My God,' he said. 'You sound like the bloody police. I don't suppose you've got a warrant?'

George was about to say that under the Wildlife and Countryside Act he did not need a warrant if he had sufficient evidence that a crime had been committed, but never found out if Williams would have believed the bluff. Pritchard appeared out of the mist at the end of the track, his raincoat flapping around his knees. He looked angry and exhausted. As he approached up the track George could see splashes of mud on his face and a graze across his forehead.

'I lost him,' he said. 'He must have left the road somewhere and gone back on to the moor.' He looked at Williams with disgust. 'You're in deep trouble,' he said. 'Give your car keys to Mr Palmer-Jones and get in the back with me. We're going to the nearest police station.'

'He can't drive my car,' Williams said, his voice for the first time showing real emotion.

Pritchard said nothing. He took the keys from the man's pocket and threw them to George.

Williams sat calmly in an interview room, while Pritchard raised the sleepy, red-bricked police station to frenzy. He had walked in as if he owned the place, filling the space with his ringing tones, shouting for tea, a change of clothes, an interview room. The policemen there were already bemused by his radio call. Who was this mad Welshman from the south who arrested respectable local businessmen and caused chaos in the district with his demands for roadblocks and extra men?

'You can't arrest him!' the station sergeant had said. 'Most of the police committee go to his evening classes. He takes them out for walks on the hills.'

'He had a suspected murderer in his car.'

'Are you sure, sir?' The station sergeant was sceptical. 'Could you really see in that light? It might have been anyone.'

'It was Oliver!' Pritchard boomed, but even George could sense the trace of uncertainty in his voice. George stood quietly, a little embarrassed by Pritchard's loudness, embarrassed because he should not be there at all. He was superfluous now. This was a murder investigation and Pritchard would want to interview Williams with one of his colleagues. But Pritchard seemed determined to ignore all propriety. Perhaps he even wanted to provoke the duty sergeant to further disapproval.

'This is Mr Palmer-Jones,' he said. 'He's a Wildlife Act Inspector. I don't understand about these bloody birds so he's sitting in on the interview in case I need him. Can you arrange for some tea? And find out all there is to know about Williams.'

Pritchard and George stood for a moment in the corridor and watched Williams through the interview room door. It seemed to George that he seemed surprisingly at home there.

'Has he got a record?' he asked.

'As long as your arm,' Pritchard said. 'But all spent convictions and mostly as a juvenile. He came from a very respectable family and they threw him out when he first got into trouble. That was in the early sixties and work was easy to find. He moved around a lot, mixed with a lot of nasty customers, usually got caught. Then he came back like the prodigal son and hasn't been in trouble since. Apparently they think a lot of him in the district.'

'He's not been involved with the police at all?'

Pritchard shook his head. 'He's not even had a parking ticket for his precious car,' he said. 'He's done a lot of charitable work in Puddleworth and the surrounding area. He's never hidden his record, in fact he's made quite a feature of it in the publicity. You know the sort of thing – he reformed and became successful, so with a bit of help so could all the other bad lads in the town.'

'Do you think he's reformed?' George asked.

'Perhaps,' Pritchard said. 'Or perhaps he just got clever and changed his field of operation.'

They went in. Theo Williams was sitting upright on the plastic chair with his palms flat on the table before him. The cuffs of his jacket had slipped back over his wrists, so they could see the gold watch and gold cuff links. He might have been born in the country, George thought, but there was something of the city wise boy about him. He was about forty, round-faced, fleshy. He took great care of himself.

Pritchard sat on the other side of the table from the man. George took the seat in a corner where a constable had been sitting before they came into the room.

'Now,' Pritchard said. 'Tell me about Frank Oliver.'

'I'm sorry, Superintendent,' Williams said. 'I'm afraid there must be some mistake. I haven't seen Frank Oliver for weeks.' In his time alone in the interview room he had composed himself and decided to be polite. It was clever, George thought, to admit to knowing Oliver.

'Who was in your car this morning, Mr Williams?'

'I don't know, Superintendent. Really, I don't know.' He gave a little gesture of helplessness as if to show that he was devastated that he could not supply Pritchard with more information. 'I picked up a hitch hiker on the way from Puddleworth. I was going to take him all the way to Shrewsbury. Perhaps he got fed up while I went for a walk.'

'You told Mr Palmer-Jones there was no one in the car.'

Williams smiled and showed the gold in his teeth.

'I don't like officials,' he said. 'I think they should mind their own business. It was an instinctive reaction to lie.'

'Do you usually walk on the hill in this weather so early in the morning?'

'I'm interested in birds of prey, Mr Pritchard,' Williams said. 'I've been studying merlins in this area for many years.'

He smiled again.

'How well do you know Oliver?' Pritchard asked. 'He's a falconer,'

Williams said. 'A very good falconer.' He flexed his fingers. He had long, woman's hands. 'I work quite closely with falconers. I prepare skins of birds of prey for exhibition. We met through Mr Fenn at the Puddleworth Centre.'

'Tell me about your interest in taxidermy,' said Pritchard. 'How did that begin?'

'My father was a gamekeeper,' Williams said. 'I grew up learning about wildlife and the countryside. Then when I was at borstal we had a talk from a local taxidermist. I was hooked. When I got out I was taken on as an apprentice at a big place in north London. I started off scraping elephants' trunks and preparing rhino feet umbrella stands, but I loved it. Eventually I had my own workshop in the craft centre at Puddleworth. I can tell you, Superintendent, that without my interest I might be a hardened criminal by now.'

Pritchard leaned forward across the table.

'I think you and Oliver were partners,' he said. 'I think you had trouble getting dead birds to stuff so you started taking them from the wild. Then you found that Oliver was doing the same thing but he was selling the birds to falconers so you went into business together, sharing your information.'

'That's slanderous, Mr Pritchard,' Williams said. 'I've a lot of powerful friends. I hope you've some evidence for those allegations.'

Pritchard ignored the interruption and continued: 'Then Oliver cocked up your nice little scheme, didn't he? He was stealing the Sarne peregrines – a special order because of their historical significance – when someone frightened him. He lost his head and killed an old lady. That was very careless.'

'You're being ridiculous, Superintendent,' Williams said. 'You can have no reason to suppose that Oliver and I had any business connection. We're acquaintances with a similar interest, nothing more.' He sounded supremely confident, but he had taken a cigarette from a packet and lit it with a kind of nervous desperation.

'Can't we?' Pritchard said. 'How do you think we knew where to find you today?'

The policeman looked apologetically at George. 'Look,' he said expansively, 'I don't care about these birds. It doesn't matter to me. I'm not going to pursue that line of inquiry if you help me. I want to find a murderer. Tell me where Frank Oliver is and we can all go home.'

But Williams had become tight-lipped and stubborn.

'I'm sorry, Superintendent,' he said. 'I can't help you. Now if you've nothing to charge me with I think you should let me go. I'm a busy man.'

George could tell that Pritchard was in a difficult position. Williams was a prominent man in the community – parish councillor, chairman of the Rotary club, school governor. Without substantial proof it would be hard for him to detain the man. Williams sensed triumph and began to rise to his feet. Then there was a knock at the door and a constable passed a slip of paper to the superintendent. He looked at it blankly, then beckoned George to follow him into the corridor.

'I don't understand a word of this,' he said. 'Does it mean anything to you, George?'

George looked at the paper. It was a message from the RSPB Regional Officer.

'I told you,' he said, 'that the RSPB warden didn't see Mr Williams at the merlins' nest and that the eggs weren't in his possession when Lewis found him. This note says that Lewis has found the eggs in a rucksack behind the drystone wall by the track.' He looked through the glass door at Williams, 'I don't think a natural predator would be clever enough to hide the eggs in a rucksack,' he said.

'That's all very well,' Pritchard said. 'But what does it all mean?'

'It means,' George said, 'that you have sufficient evidence to charge Mr Williams with wilful disturbance of a schedule one species and theft of its eggs.'

Pritchard beamed and opened the door into the interview room.

'You'd better sit down Mr Williams,' he said. 'It's going to be a long day.'

Chapter Eight

Williams' taxidermist workshop was part of a craft centre in some converted farm buildings in Puddleworth village near to the green. Williams had been bailed on the charge under the Wildlife and Countryside Act. He had agreed, reluctantly, to allow his car to stay at the police station to be fingerprinted, and had accepted Pritchard's offer of a lift home. He had steadfastly refused to answer any further questions about Oliver and maintained his story that he had picked up a hitch hiker on his way to Shrewsbury. When Pritchard had asked permission to search the workshop, Williams had said smoothly that he was a decent citizen and he would do all he could to assist the police. Of course they could look round the workshop. He had nothing to hide. He hoped they would be discreet. He had a living to make.

There were eight different units in the craft centre built round the cobbled farmyard. Each had a large semicircular window displaying goods for sale and a workshop behind, where the public could watch work in progress. The place was attractive and well-advertised and at the weekends it was very busy. People came out from Wolverhampton and Birmingham to spend an afternoon in the country and to buy the over-priced goods. Upstairs, in the main building, above the pottery and the stripped pine furniture, there was a café selling wholemeal quiche and home-made cakes and a shop full of arty gifts.

The centre had few visitors that afternoon. The day was overcast, though the cloud had lifted so that they could see the long bank of hills to the west which towered above the village, restricting the horizon. To the east was a wood, then the flat plain to the city, but there was no view from the centre.

Pritchard parked his car under the dripping trees in the car park by the road and they walked to Williams' workshop. On the way past a unit where two women designed and hand-knitted sweaters, Williams was accosted by one of the occupants. She ran out into the yard and held on to his arm. She was tall, with very long, black hair twisted into individual curls. She wore black stretch trousers and one of her own creations – a large mohair sweater in a geometric black and red design.

'Theo,' she said in a painful Birmingham accent, 'I'm glad I've caught you. I want to talk to you about this evening's meeting.'

It seemed that the craft centre was run by a management committee of the workshop owners and she wanted his support for a proposal of her own.

'I'm sorry,' he said brusquely. 'You can see I'm busy. I can't stop now.'

The hand held more tightly to his jacket sleeve. 'It's no good running away, Theo. When you took over the workshop you agreed to participate in the committee. We've got to discuss it now.'

It was the sort of argument a married couple might have, George thought. He suspected there was some greater intimacy between them than that they shared the running of the centre. She seemed to have some claim on him and to be afraid of losing him.

'That's all right, sir,' Pritchard said. 'We don't want to disturb you more than we can help. Give us a key and we'll let ourselves in. You can join us when you've completed your business with this young lady.'

Williams looked at him angrily, but gave him the key. Pritchard and George walked on. The woman dragged Williams into her shop and continued to talk to him.

The whole of Williams' shop window was arranged as a woodland scene. There were dead leaves on the floor, and branches and a hollow log formed a background. Against this the mounted birds and animals were set in a display. There were a fox, a pheasant and a group of partridges. Pritchard stared at it with a child's curiosity.

'Who would want to buy that sort of thing?' he asked.

George shrugged. 'Some people find them attractive. There seems to be a market, especially among people involved in country sports.'

Pritchard unlocked the door into the display area. More stuffed birds stood in glass cabinets. Most it seemed were not for sale, but were waiting to be sent back to the sportsmen who had provided the skins for mounting. Pritchard's colleagues had already been into the place to look for Oliver's fingerprints and there were a series of muddy footprints on the red quarry-tile floor. Williams' workshop was behind a low, hinged counter, so he could speak to anyone who came into the shop and they could watch him working. He would sit at a wooden bench against one wall and the tools of his craft were set out there. There was a faint smell of chemicals, of borax and wood wool. Williams was in the process of mounting a buzzard. The viscera had been removed and the skin was rolled up, turned inside out around the buzzard's head like a strange collar. A piece of wire had been stuck into the bone at the base of the bird's skull and at the other end, into the bone at the base of the tail. The wire was wound round and round with wood wool to recreate the bulk of the bird's body. Its head was stuffed with cotton wool. Another wire had been twisted at right angles to the first. When the skin was unrolled, this would support the wings.

'Williams must have been called away suddenly,' George said. 'He would never have chosen to leave the skin like that. He's in the middle of a very delicate operation.'

Pritchard went up to the workbench, fascinated. The bird's feet were still there. A wire from the body would go through the hollow legs into a wooden block, so that eventually the buzzard would stand in someone's collection. There were scalpels, a wad of cotton wool and reels of wire of different thickness.

'What's to stop Williams killing wild birds, mounting them and selling them?' Pritchard asked.

'A taxidermist is supposed to have a licence showing the origin of each bird he sells,' George said, 'but I'm sure there are ways round that.'

'Let's see what else he's got here,' Pritchard said. 'We need the names and addresses of other people who might be harbouring Oliver.' He moved restlessly around the small room, opening cupboards and pulling out drawers, but found nothing to interest him.

George wandered into a scullery behind the workshop, where there was a stainless steel sink and draining board and a large freezer. Inside, as he had expected, was a pile of frozen corpses. There were a badger and a fox and several tawny owls but most were gamebirds: woodcock, snipe and red grouse. There was also a small male peregrine, very grey and fine. George wondered if it were some falconer's favourite bird which had met with an accident, or if it had been taken from the wild. He presumed there were records somewhere to show its origin. Williams had seemed very confident that they would find everything in order. He closed the freezer lid.

Pritchard called from the workshop: 'let's go upstairs and look round his flat before he comes back. We might have more luck there.' George followed him slowly up the dark, narrow wooden stairs.

The flat was small and furnished in a fussy, almost feminine way. Williams might have chosen the design from a popular women's magazine. He had obviously taken care with the decorating and in choosing the furniture, but the place felt impersonal, as if it were hardly lived in. George thought that Williams had not the confidence to choose what he really liked and probably did not feel at ease there himself. He would be more relaxed in the workshop downstairs. The bedroom was just big enough for a double bed and a pine wardrobe. The living room had a glass-topped table and two upright chairs and a small settee with flowered cream covers. There were spot lights and an expensive stereo system. Pritchard sat at the table and began to look through the address book he had found near the white, push-button telephone.

'What would you like me to do?' George asked. He was feeling tired. He wished he had his own transport so he could return to Gorse Hill. This was police constable's work. He could be using his time more effectively.

'Look for a shotgun,' Pritchard said distractedly. George might have been one of his subordinates. During the day he had lost the attitude of polite deference he had assumed at the beginning of the inquiry. 'He's got a shotgun licence apparently but I didn't see the thing downstairs and the lads who were here earlier didn't mention it.'

There were not many places to search. Under the bed George found a pile of pornographic magazines. The wardrobe was only just big enough for the profusion of clothes. In a drawer under the wardrobe he found a passport which showed that Williams had made regular trips to Europe and Scandinavia. He carried it through to the living room and showed it to Pritchard.

'Look at this,' he said. 'It's possible that Williams was making legitimate business trips, but he might be illegally exporting some of the birds he and Oliver took. It could explain the conversation between Oliver and his son in the Hop Pole. Perhaps they were hoping to recruit Stephen as a courier.'

'Perhaps they were,' Pritchard said. 'But it doesn't help us to find Oliver.'

The phone rang, interrupting his depression. With a sudden optimism he leapt to his feet. 'Perhaps they've found him,' he said. But when he answered the phone he showed no great happiness. He listened, answered briefly and replaced the receiver.

'That shopping list of birds which we found in Oliver's house was typed on the machine in Fenn's office,' he said. 'They asked Fenn to type them a sample.'

'So it could have been typed by Oliver,' George said. 'It seems unlikely.'

'I still think Fenn is implicated,' Pritchard said. 'It's too much of a coincidence to think he knew nothing about it. Williams and Fenn are practically neighbours and Oliver works there. Fenn must have had some idea what was going on. I wouldn't be surprised if he knows where Oliver is. He's probably behind the whole organization.'

'Perhaps,' George said. He found it hard to reconcile Pritchard's image of Fenn as a ruthless criminal with his knowledge of the man. It seemed to him that Fenn was too nervous, too sad to organize the theft and sale of the birds of prey. Yet the modern, well-equipped Falconry Centre had been paid for somehow, and Fenn had been obsessed with his dream of founding a place where he could show his birds to their best advantage.

Outside, they heard the grating Birmingham accent of the knitwear designer, still reluctant to let Williams go.

'You will be there, Theo,' she said. 'It's a very important meeting.'

They did not hear Williams' reply, but soon after the door of the shop banged and there were footsteps on the stairs.

'You've made yourselves at home then,' he said unpleasantly as he came into the living room. The conversation with the woman seemed to have irritated him beyond reason.

'Yes sir,' Pritchard said. 'Thank you very much for your cooperation. We won't hold you up much longer. We'll let you get back to that bird downstairs. I've just a few more questions. Where's your shotgun?'

Williams seemed surprised by the question.

'Wasn't it in the car?' he asked sharply.

Pritchard shook his head. 'Was it in the car when you went out this morning?' he said.

Williams seemed unsure how to answer. 'I thought it was,' he blustered. 'Perhaps I was mistaken.'

'If you gave it to Oliver,' Pritchard said, 'you're more of a fool than I thought.'

'I didn't give anything to Oliver, Superintendent. I've already told you. I haven't seen him for weeks.'

But he seemed worried, anxious.

'Of course,' Pritchard said. 'Oliver might have taken the gun without your permission while you were walking on the hill.' He paused and turned to Palmer-Jones. 'I had an idea this morning,' he said, 'that Oliver was carrying something.' He returned his gaze to Williams. 'We're going to catch him eventually,' he said. 'If he's armed with your shotgun when we do you're going to be in real trouble.'

George thought for a moment that Williams would speak. The logic of Pritchard's argument seemed to have frightened him. But a deeper fear, or stubbornness, prevented him.

'I'm not listening to these fairy stories,' he said. 'I've work to do.' But at the top of the stairs he paused. He wanted them out of his home. 'Are you ready to leave?' he asked.

Pritchard seemed reluctant to go. He was walking up and down the small room as if he hoped to gain inspiration from the stuffed tawny owl on the window sill, the photograph of the peregrine on eggs above the mantelpiece.

'Yes,' he said in the end. 'We'll pass on these addresses to the local lads and then we'll go back to Sarne.'

With any luck, he thought, he would be home by the boys' bathtime. He loved the riotous ritual of bubbles, splashing, the boys in the tub together as wriggling and slippery as tadpoles. He gave the room a final glance and Williams started heavily down the stairs.

George was last out of the room so when the phone began to ring, he turned back to answer it. He had expected it to be another message for Pritchard and was surprised when he heard a woman's voice, expressionless as a machine. There was an overseas reversed-charges call, she said, from a town in Holland for Mr Williams. Was he prepared to take it? George put his hand over the receiver and shouted to Pritchard. The operator repeated her question. Yes, George said. Yes, he was prepared to accept the call. Pritchard took the receiver but held it so that George could listen too. Williams, confused and indignant, muttering about the invasion of his privacy, came back up the stairs and into the room. George recognized the voice at the end of the telephone at once, but could not place it until the young woman gave her name.

'Hello, Theo?' she said, clear and strident as if she were standing outside the Falconry Centre shouting to some recalcitrant schoolchild. 'This is Kerry. I've decided to keep out of the way for a bit until the fuss dies down. We don't want the police to make any unfortunate connections between us.' There was a pause. She was obviously expecting some response. 'Theo?' she said, a note of anxiety in her voice. 'Are you there, Theo?'

'I'm sorry, Miss Fenn,' Pritchard said. 'Mr Williams isn't at home at present. Perhaps you'd like to talk to us.'

Kerry Fenn swore at him and the phone went dead.

The car park at the Falconry Centre was full. The press reports of an elderly lady pecked to death by a giant hawk had done nothing to frighten visitors away. The people came in droves and there was a queue outside the aviary where the red-tailed hawk was kept. When George and Pritchard asked at the turnstile to speak to Mr Fenn, the cashier thought they were reporters and would not let them through without paying. She had the untidy appearance and high moral tone of a vicar's wife.

'Mr Fenn's very distressed about what happened to Mrs Masefield,' she said, 'but the police have made it quite clear that her death had nothing to do with the Puddleworth birds of prey. I think you should leave him alone.'

Pritchard paid his two pounds and said nothing. It seemed unlikely now that he would be back in Sarne in time to bath the boys. He thought again of Williams' reaction to Kerry Fenn's phone call. The man had begun to sweat, so that the round, highly coloured face had seemed glossy, plastic like a mask.

'Tell me,' Pritchard had said, 'about your connections with Kerry Fenn. Does she employ you and Oliver? She mixes in all the right circles, doesn't she? She typed the shopping list of birds and gave it to Oliver, so you would both know exactly which species to take.'

But Williams had smiled suggestively, so that the plastic mask turned into a leer.

'My only connection with Kerry Fenn is purely personal, Superintendent,' he said. 'I can give you details of that if you want me to, but I think it might shock your elderly friend here.'

And he had stuck to his story that his relationship with Kerry was physical. She had fancied him, he said. She had a Lady Chatterley fantasy. What was he do to? They had kept it secret because her father would have disapproved. It seemed more likely to Pritchard that the fantasy was Williams' but the taxidermist would not change his story, and as they left he gave them a triumphant smile.

They found Fenn in the office of his bungalow. He looked grey and tired. He saw them through the window coming down the path from the Centre and got up to meet them at the door.

'I'm busy,' he said. 'Kerry usually does the books but she's away. I'm not so good with figures as she is.' But the attempt to refuse them entry was half-hearted and he sighed and let them into the house. 'I can't give you very long,' he said. 'I'm doing a display at half past three.'

The three men stood uneasily in the hall.

'Shall we go into the kitchen?' Pritchard said gently. 'We'll be more comfortable there.'

Fenn led them into the big kitchen and they perched ridiculously on high stools by a built-in bar, like three garden gnomes.

'Would you like some coffee?' Fenn asked, but Pritchard shook his head.

'What do you know about Theo Williams?' he asked.

'He's a taxidermist based in the village here,' Fenn said. 'He has rather a good reputation. He prepared some of our displays in the visitors' centre.'

'Is he interested in birds of prey?'

'He seems to be. His father was a gamekeeper. Theo used to go out with him and learned from him, I suppose. He's not a falconer.'

'Are Williams and Oliver friendly?'

'I don't know. I don't think they particularly like each other but Williams comes here occasionally to talk to Frank Oliver.' Fenn paused. 'I don't suppose it matters,' he said, 'that Oliver's got himself into more serious trouble now but I used to think they might have had some business connection. Williams used to go shooting with his father when the old man was still alive. He probably sees some of the schedule one birds of prey as fair game and I expect Oliver has been able to find a market for the mounted skins.'

Pritchard turned helplessly to George.

'I'm afraid,' George said, 'the business connection between Williams and Oliver is rather more serious than that.'

'I'm sorry,' Fenn said. 'I don't understand you.' He stared out of the window as if he had lost interest in the conversation. Throughout the conversation George felt Fenn's attention wandering as if he were a very old man or a child.

'Oliver and Williams work together,' George said. 'They steal eggs and young birds of prey from the wild to sell to falconers. We're sure now that some of the birds were smuggled abroad for sale. That's why Oliver was on the hill at Sarne on the day of Eleanor's murder.'

'I see,' Fenn said absently. 'Yes. I see.'

'We don't believe Williams and Oliver are working alone,' George said. 'We think they're employed by someone with a greater organizational skill, someone perhaps who has legitimate business abroad.

'I can understand that,' Fenn said, showing for the first time that he was following the line of George's argument. 'Neither Frank Oliver nor Williams is very bright.'

George paused, hoping perhaps that Pritchard would take over the explanation, but the policeman motioned for him to continue.

'Where is your daughter, Mr Fenn?' George asked.

'Mm?' Fenn looked up, startled from his daydreams by the question.

'Where is Kerry?' George repeated.

'Oh she's in Holland,' he said. 'We're hoping to import some birds from a centre there.'

'Does she go abroad quite often?'

'Yes,' he said. 'She's good at that side of things and she seems to enjoy it. I'm very lucky.' Still he did not grasp the implication of the questions. 'What has Kerry to do with Theo Williams and Frank Oliver?'

'We think she may be employing them,' George said. 'We think she finds the buyers for the birds. She has met influential falconers here and abroad. As you've said she's good at organization. She tells the men what to steal and disposes of the eggs and young when they're delivered.'

Fenn began to laugh, a sad, wracking, crazy laugh which shook his body like a cough.

'She's a girl,' he said, 'a pretty, sweet girl. You're mad.'

Pritchard took the flimsy shopping list of birds from a file. 'This was typed on the machine in your office,' he said. 'We found it in Oliver's house.'

Fenn looked at it suspiciously.

'That doesn't mean anything,' he said. 'Oliver could have typed it himself.'

'I don't think so,' Pritchard said. 'You told us when we were last here that Mr Oliver didn't have access to your home.'

'I don't care what you say,' Fenn said. 'Kerry takes after her mother. Lydia would never do anything that wasn't honest and decent.'

He put his head in his hands and seemed deep in memory.

'Is Kerry friendly with Theo Williams?' George asked quietly. 'Do they go out together socially?'

'Of course not!' Fenn was jerked back to the present by the horror of the suggestion. 'I suppose the chap's all right. He got himself into trouble in the past, though I understand that's all over now. But he has nothing in common with my daughter. The idea's ludicrous.'

'We were in Williams' flat just now,' George said, 'when Kerry telephoned him from Holland.'

'That's impossible,' Fenn said. 'She wouldn't have done that. He must have been lying.'

'I spoke to her.' George said.

'Then you must have made a mistake.'

'No,' George said. Fenn was fighting not to convince them but to sustain his own belief in his daughter's virtue and perfection. Without that he had nothing. But eventually he would have to realize the truth. 'No,' George said. 'I couldn't have been mistaken. Kerry gave her name and I recognized her voice as soon as she spoke.'

Fenn said nothing. He had heard the words but refused to accept what George was saying.

'Williams was with us in the flat when the telephone rang,' George went on. 'Of course we asked him why Kerry would want to phone him at home. He insisted that he and your daughter were intimately involved with each other, that they were lovers.'

'No,' Fenn said. His face was white and the shock seemed to have cleared his head of all confusion. 'He was lying to save himself. Kerry has grace and taste. She would never be attracted to him.'

'In that case,' Pritchard said cheerfully, sliding off his stool, 'they must be business partners. There's really no other explanation. I'm afraid, Mr Fenn, I'm going to have to ask you to let me search her room.'

Fenn nodded and led them down a long corridor to a large bedroom at the end of the bungalow. 'You'll see,' he said with one last burst of resistance. 'You'll see that she has nothing to hide.' But then he retreated again into his own thoughts as if the present were too painful to bear, and although Pritchard put more questions to him he did not answer.

The room, like the rest of the house, was modern and airy and without character. It was like the bedroom in an expensive hotel – it was pleasantly furnished and decorated but it gave nothing of its occupant away. French windows led on to a paved yard and looked out over farmland. There were fitted wardrobes along one wall and a large bed with wooden spindle headboard.

It seemed suddenly to George that he had spent all day searching through other people's underwear, other people's intimate lives, and he felt sickened. He longed for it all to be over so they could go home. Let Pritchard do his own dirty work, he thought, and stood next to Fenn while the policeman began to look through drawers and cupboards. He found what he was looking for quite quickly. There was a buff envelope file in her small bedside cupboard under a pile of paperback novels. There was nothing written on the outside of the file, but immediately inside there was an exact copy of the shopping list they had found in Oliver's home.

'There you are,' Pritchard said. 'That proves it. That's what we were looking for.'

'But it's another carbon copy,' George said quietly. 'Where's the original?'

Pritchard shrugged. All this was a side issue. He wanted to find Oliver. Nothing else mattered much. 'Perhaps Williams has it somewhere,' he said. 'We didn't search his place that well.'

He began to spread the other papers from the file over the bed. They were all copies of letters. Some acknowledged receipt of orders for eggs or young birds, and requested half payment in advance. Others were receipts for money paid.

'I wonder where she keeps the accounts,' Pritchard said. 'There must be some record of the money paid out to Oliver and Williams and of the payment received.'

He gathered the papers together and pushed them back into the file.

'We'll have to take these with us,' he said to Fenn. 'You understand that?'

Fenn nodded.

George realized that there was still a small white card on the bed. Pritchard had tipped it out of the file, but missed it when he gathered the flimsies together. George picked it up and turned it over, so he could see what was written on the other side. It was a business card: Gorse Hill Country Hotel, Sarne, printed tastefully in gold, followed by the hotel's telephone number.

'Is there any reason why Kerry would have the telephone number at Gorse Hill?' George asked Murdoch Fenn.

The falconer shook his head. He was too shocked to think or to care. George remembered the slip of paper they had found in Oliver's concrete cell. That too had the telephone number of Gorse Hill written on it. They had assumed that Oliver had kept it to contact his wife in an emergency, but perhaps it had some other significance. Perhaps after all the answer to Eleanor's death lay in Sarne.

Pritchard took the card from George and slipped it into the file without looking at it. He turned to Fenn. 'Has your daughter any special friends?' he asked. 'Someone who may be hiding Frank Oliver?'

'Kerry doesn't have many friends,' Fenn said. 'She's too busy at work.'

'You haven't a holiday home, a cottage or chalet?'

'No,' Fenn said. 'All our profit goes back into the Falconry Centre.'

'Well then,' Pritchard said, 'I don't think I need trouble you any longer.' He looked at his watch. With luck they would not be too late back after all.

As they were leaving the bungalow the middle-aged cashier was coming down the path towards them, her grey hair blowing in the wind.

'Oh Mr Fenn,' she said. 'You haven't forgotten the display at half past three? The children are waiting.'

She sounded anxious and a little irritated, like a mother whose favourite child is always late.

'No,' he said absently. 'No I haven't forgotten. Excuse me, gentlemen.'

He hurried up the path away from them and as they made their way back to their car they saw him in the display field. He was a small, pathetic figure made dignified and rather sinister by the powerful bird held on his arm.

Chapter Nine

That morning Molly woke to a gloomy half light and the sound of rainwater gurgling in drain pipes. It was very early. She imagined George waiting on the moor for some mysterious stranger to come out of the mist, intent on stealing a clutch of merlins' eggs. It still seemed to her that the men's antics on Farthing Ridge would be a wild-goose chase, a lunacy. What was George trying to prove? Was he trying to exorcize his guilt for Eleanor's death by getting soaked to the skin? What could some stranger on the moor have to do with Eleanor Masefield?

Molly found it impossible to go back to sleep. She remembered Eleanor and wondered if her dislike of the woman exaggerated the image she conjured in her head. It seemed to her now that Eleanor had dominated her family ruthlessly. She had purposely made them dependent on her, financially and emotionally. Their home and their livelihood depended on her. The small, beautiful woman had refused to relinquish control over her daughter and grandchildren, and they had only gained freedom with her death. That seemed more real and fundamental than the cartoon-like adventures of evil falconers and the brave heroes who sat in the rain to catch them. Molly lay awake in the big cold bed and struggled to make sense of it all. It would never have been necessary before. She had always trusted George's logic. George would have made lists, made connections. But here his judgement was clouded and the responsibility was hers. She felt like a woman who had always relied on her husband to mend the car, stranded with a puncture on a lonely road.

Molly had told Helen, the night before, about the discussion in the Hop Pole about passports.

'I've told my husband,' she said. 'He will have passed the information to the police.'

The girl had seemed excited and intrigued and promised to tell Laurie.

'And Mrs Oliver,' Molly had prompted. 'You should tell her.'

'Of course,' Helen said. 'I'm not going to school tomorrow. They told Father we could have a few days at home. So if you need any help . . .'

And it was Helen, dressed in jeans and a striped shirt, who brought Molly's breakfast.

'Did you see Mrs Oliver last night?' Molly asked. 'No,' Helen said. 'I didn't even see Laurie. They're not on the phone. I'm going there this morning.'

'Mrs Oliver isn't here today?'

'Not yet,' Helen said. 'But she is coming. Father wanted her to stay at home until she had some news of Steve but she wanted to come in to work. She said she was better if she was busy.'

'Sit down,' Molly said, 'and tell me about your grandmother.'

Helen sat and talked. Her love for Laurie, or perhaps her perceived triumph over Nan Oliver, had seemed to have given her a new strength and confidence. She spoke and moved more spontaneously. She gave her opinion without any of the old shyness. Molly had never known her so animated.

'She was autocratic,' Helen said. 'My mother and father would never stand up to her and that made her worse. Mother was frightened of her of course, and at the same time she needed her. Mother didn't dare sneeze without asking Grandmother first. Father wasn't scared of her but he wouldn't confront her because it made Mother so nervous. Eleanor pretended not to like Father, just to upset her. Eleanor said that Mother had married beneath her and that Father was petty and boring, but she didn't mean it. She didn't mind him being petty and boring when it came to dealing with Inland Revenue and the VAT man.'

It seemed to Molly that Helen had watched the tension within her family and had been helpless to do anything about it. Now at last she could talk about it without making her mother even more vulnerable.

'Eleanor must have been hard to live with,' Molly said.

'She was,' said Helen. 'Dreadfully. The worst thing was that she always assumed she knew what was best for us. It was worse for Fanny. Grandmother was always nagging her about being overweight and not having the right sort of friends. In lots of ways it was easier for me but she still thought she knew what was best for me. She liked me. She said I was her natural successor and that I should have to take over the business. Mother and Father were too soft, she said, and Fanny was too stupid. When I left school she would train me to take control. That's what I mean. She assumed that when I left school I would want to come and work for her. When I said that I had applied to go to university she seemed astounded. She had taken it for granted I would do as she expected. It took a lot of nerve to tell her. She could be intimidating even to her favourites.'

'What did your grandmother say when you told her that you wanted to go to university?'

'That she supposed another three years wouldn't do any harm and we could make a start in the long holidays. As I've said she just assumed that I'd come into the hotel.'

'And will you?' Molly asked. 'Will you work at the hotel with your parents when you've finished at university?'

'I don't know yet,' Helen said. 'And if I do it will be my decision.'

Molly remembered the shy, mouse-like girl Helen had seemed to be before Eleanor's death. Would it have been your decision, she thought, if Eleanor were still alive?

'What will you do today?' Helen asked. She was on her feet and had begun to collect the dirty plates.

'I'll have a quiet day here,' Molly said, 'and wait for George to come home.'

Poor thing, Helen thought. How dreadful to belong to a generation which can do nothing but wait for their husbands! She left Molly alone. Molly sat, pretending to read the paper, and thinking, until mid morning, when she went to look for Veronica. Richard Mead was sitting in the office with the door open, talking on the telephone.

'I'm sorry,' he was saying. 'We're not taking any bookings this week.'

The person on the other end of the telephone must have tried to persuade him to allow them to stay.

'I'm sorry,' he repeated. 'Mrs Masefield is dead. I'm afraid we won't be able to accommodate you.'

He replaced the receiver, and waved to Molly.

'I'm looking for Veronica,' she said. 'Have you seen her?'

'She's in the conservatory, I think,' he said and turned back to his work.

'Of course,' Veronica said, 'Mother always said that I'd married beneath me.'

They were sitting in the conservatory on the white-painted wicker chairs, watching the drizzle mist the glass. They could see nothing outside. Molly had listened to Veronica's confessions before, but never so intently. She had let the words wash over her. Now she drank coffee and nodded with the same attitude of accepting sympathy, but she was listening. 'It wasn't true,' Veronica was saying. 'Mother knew really how lucky I was to find Richard. I never did very well at school. I only got the job in an estate agent's office because Mother was friendly with the manager. If I hadn't married I'm sure they would have sacked me. It wasn't as if we had very much money, even when Father was alive. He was very extravagant. I don't know how we managed at all. He never seemed to do any work.'

'So Eleanor never approved of Richard?' Molly said.

'She didn't approve of his family,' Veronica said. 'Richard's father was a farmer, quite wealthy at one time, but he went bankrupt. He was a drunk and they never knew where he was. It must have been a terrible ordeal for Richard and his mother. His father had to go to court and everyone was talking about it. Richard's never forgotten it. That's why he cares so much about our girls. He never had any security when he was a child. Mother saw the bankruptcy as a great disgrace. She always enjoyed other people's misfortune.'

'What did your father think of your marriage?'

'He'd given up on me by then,' Veronica said, 'because I wasn't academic. I don't think he cared very much who I married so long as it didn't disturb him. It might have been different if I were a boy. I tried to be interested in birds of prey to please him but he thought I was too silly to understand.'

That reminded Molly suddenly of the phone call she had taken the day before.

'Who is Kerry Fenn?' she asked. 'Is she any relative of Murdoch Fenn, the falconer?'

'I don't know,' Veronica said. She was absorbed in herself, in her memories, her resentment of her mother and her attachment to her. 'I think he had a daughter but I can't remember her name.'

'Someone phoned yesterday afternoon,' Molly said. 'A foreigner. He said it was business and that Kerry Fenn had told him to contact Gorse Hill. Perhaps I should have told George when he phoned.'

'We have lots of foreign visitors,' Veronica said absently. 'They come because they like the countryside. It's so typically English.'

Veronica was typically English too, Molly thought, with her cashmere sweater and her sensible shoes and her soft, unassuming prettiness. As she had with Helen, Molly had the feeling that Veronica was experiencing a new freedom. She was frightened of it, and would probably transfer her dependence from her mother to her husband, but perhaps he would encourage her to be stronger, more confident.

'How did Fanny and Helen get on with Eleanor?' Molly asked. Veronica poured herself another cup of coffee, sipped at it.

'She and Fanny were always arguing,' she said. 'Fanny's at a difficult age of course. I'm sure she would have grown out of it. It worried Richard. He said I should talk to Mother and tell her to leave Fanny alone, but I always found that sort of thing difficult.'

'And Helen?'

'Mother liked Helen,' Veronica said, and Molly thought she sensed a note of jealousy, as if she had been in competition with her elder daughter for Eleanor's affection. 'Mother said Helen was bright. She had high hopes for her.'

'Did those high hopes include marriage?' Molly asked.

'No,' Veronica said slowly. 'I don't think she would have wanted Helen to marry. She would have wanted Helen here at Gorse Hill, to be a credit to her, to be her audience, so that they could be charming together.'

Molly looked at the vacant face, startled, surprised by the bitterness in the woman's voice.

Richard Mead had offered to collect Nan Oliver in the car to take her to Gorse Hill, but because of pride and a stubborn perversity she had refused and said she preferred to walk. It was just as well that she had, she thought, as she stood by the side of the lane and watched Frank, furtive and ridiculous, climb out of the dripping gorse bush. His wet hair was stuck to his forehead.

'Where's Steve?' she asked.

'He's safe,' he said. 'Even if they catch him he can prove he had nothing to do with the old lady's death.'

She stood, legs slightly apart, staring at him, taking pleasure in his wet discomfort.

'Well,' he demanded. 'Are you going to help me?'

'I don't know,' she said. 'Why should I?'

Then he began to talk in an earnest whisper, although there was no one at all to hear them. She knew she would help him. She owed him no favours, but if it came to a choice between him and the family at Gorse Hill she knew where her loyalties lay. He was one of her sort.

He disappeared back into the hedge like an animal. Although she was almost at Gorse Hill she turned down the hill and returned home. Anyone peering out of the net curtains would have assumed that she had just been into town. The policeman on the street corner acknowledged her but took no real notice. He had been told to look out for Frank, not to make a note of her comings and goings. She let herself into the house and grinned for a moment, remembering Frank's damp humiliation, as she leaned back against the front door. Then she remembered Frank's fear, the panic in his words and the gun he held loosely in one hand. There was nothing to laugh about. The house was quiet. The young ones were at school but Laurie was still there, lying on the settee, reading one of his school books. His inactivity annoyed her. He was a grown man and he spent his time lying around like one of those pampered girls at Gorse Hill. He looked up.

'I wasn't expecting you back,' he said. He sounded worried and she thought he must have arranged to meet Helen at the house. 'Is there any news?'

'No,' she said. 'I promised Mrs Mead some clothes for the WRVS and I forgot them. I'll be gone again soon.'

He was so relieved that she would be away, that he would have the house to himself when Helen arrived, that he did not notice the inconsistencies in her statement. It did not occur to him that she would never have walked most of the way back from Gorse Hill just to fetch jumble for Veronica Mead. She knew it would not do to tell him about Frank. In her mind Laurie had almost become a part of the Gorse Hill family through his association with Helen. She knew she could not trust him. He wanted only to avoid unpleasantness.

She went upstairs. In a cupboard in her room were some clothes which she had in fact promised to Veronica for the WRVS. They had belonged to her elder son before he had married and left home. She chose a pair of heavy jeans and a grey sweatshirt, some underclothes and a warm jersey, and folded them into two carrier bags. Halfway down the stairs she stopped. She went back to the bathroom, took a towel from the airing cupboard and added that to the clothes. Downstairs Laurie had put down his book and was staring blankly at the ceiling.

'What's going to happen to us all, Mum?' he said. 'I'm scared.'

I have to look after them all, she thought. Even now that they're grown up and should be looking after me. Even Frank came back to be looked after.

'It'll be all right,' she said as she had said to him many times before, as she had said to Frank. 'Just you see. Everything will be all right.'

She left the house and walked down the path to the gate with a carrier bag in each hand. She walked up the hill. The rain had soaked through the coat she had bought from a catalogue two winters before and her feet were wet. She did not stop by the gap in the hedge where Frank had been earlier that morning but carried on up the drive to Gorse Hill.

She went in through the back door and set the carrier bags down in the scullery. The kitchen was beautifully warm. She took off her coat and hung it near to the central heating boiler so it began to steam. She took a clean pink nylon overall from a drawer and put it on, doing up the buttons carefully. By then she felt more herself. She sat on the wooden chair by the boiler and took off her wet shoes. She kept slippers for working in on a shelf in the scullery and as she walked to fetch them her stockinged feet made wet footmarks on the red-tiled floor. She thought she would wash the floor. It had not been done since before the Open Day. It would give her something useful to do and take her mind off Steve and Frank.

She was standing on one foot in the scullery, pulling a flat black plastic slipper on to the other, when Richard Mead came in. He was worried about her, he said. She should have let him fetch her. Now she must sit down and get warm and let him make her some coffee. She said shortly that she had work to do and she would make herself a nice cup of tea later. Her employer went away, discouraged.

Nan Oliver was washing the kitchen floor when Molly found her. She was kneeling on a folded towel, leaning forward over the cloth, so her back was flat and parallel to the floor and the overall was stretched into wrinkles across her thighs. She had almost finished and through the hall door Molly watched her sit back on her haunches to wring out the cloth, and then stretch painfully, leaning on the kitchen table to help her, until she was standing. She turned to empty the bucket of water in the sink in the scullery and saw Molly.

'What do you want?' Nan Oliver said. 'Mrs Mead isn't here.'

'I know,' Molly said 'I've just been talking to her in the conservatory. I was looking for you.'

'You can't come in here. The floor's wet.'

'Perhaps we could talk somewhere else. Mrs Mead knows I've come to see you. She doesn't mind.'

Nan Oliver stared with reluctant admiration at the woman. She would not give in easily. And perhaps it would be dangerous to appear too hostile. Mrs Palmer-Jones might think she had something to hide.

'I've just made a pot of tea,' she said. 'We could take it into the dining room. Would you like some tea?'

'Yes,' Molly said. 'Very much.' She wondered why the woman had agreed so readily to see her. Veronica had said she would never persuade Mrs Oliver to talk. 'She's a wonder in the kitchen,' she had said, 'but a very difficult woman to get on with. Sometimes I think Eleanor only kept her on because her mother used to work with the family. Eleanor liked that sort of feudal connection.'

Mrs Oliver carried the tea into the dining room and thought that Eleanor Masefield would never have allowed one of her staff to sit there, talking to a guest. She enjoyed the thought and stretched stiff legs under the table. She poured out strong, dark tea and added plenty of sugar.

'Did you like Mrs Masefield?' Molly asked.

Nan Oliver looked at her with shrewd pale eyes. 'I don't think anyone liked her,' she said. 'Not really. Only the men. She could take in the men.'

'But you stayed on here?'

'It suited me,' Nan Oliver said. 'There isn't much work round here for a woman my age. They took me on when I came back to Sarne with my children. They didn't have to do that.'

And they paid me less than I was worth, she thought, because they knew I was desperate for work and would take anything.

'You know the police are looking for your husband?' Molly asked.

'Of course I do. I'm not daft.'

'Do you think he killed Eleanor Masefield?'

'I know that he didn't.' The woman spoke with a simple certainty.

'How could you know?'

Nan Oliver paused.

'He admired her sort,' she said at last. 'He wouldn't do anything to hurt her.'

'Her sort?'

'Gentry,' Nan Oliver said. 'People with big houses. People who fly falcons. It was all part of the same thing for him. Frank wouldn't mind making money out of them, but he wouldn't do anything to hurt them.' She spoke as if she despised his romanticism. 'He used to say Mr Masefield was a great gentleman.'

'He knew Stuart Masefield?'

'Yes. He met him at Mr Fenn's. He did some work for him every now and again. He used to come home and tell me what a lady Mrs Masefield was.'

She was sneering at Eleanor Masefield and at her husband because he was so easily impressed.

'You don't think Eleanor Masefield was a lady?' Molly asked.

Nan Oliver shrugged. 'She knew what she wanted,' she said. 'And she made sure she got it. I don't blame her, but she wasn't any different from the rest of us.'

'What do you mean? What did she want?'

'Money,' Nan Oliver said 'Power.'

'Do you know something about Eleanor Masefield which you haven't disclosed to the police?' Molly asked. But Nan Oliver refused to say any more. She had been seduced by this woman's gentle attention, by the feeling that Molly understood what she had to put up with. She had said too much already.

'I have to go now,' she said. 'I'm supposed to be working.'

Fanny slouched around the house and wished she had gone to school. The day before had been fun there. She had been the centre of attention and even the girls who usually jeered at her, or ignored her, gathered round in the cloakroom and wanted to know what had happened to Eleanor. But there had been reporters with cameras at the school gates and the headmistress and her father had decided that it would be better to stay at home for a few days. Helen did not seem to mind being banished from school. Fanny thought she was in a peculiar mood. She supposed it was because Helen was in love with Laurie Oliver. Fanny thought that if she were going to fall in love she would choose someone better than that.

She went first to the office where her father was working, dictating letters into a machine. She had thought that with Eleanor gone he would have more time for her but he seemed busier than ever. She asked if she could help him but he said that there was nothing she could do, then waited for her to go, so he could continue working. She realized during her aimless walk around the house that she would miss Eleanor. She would no longer have her grandmother to blame for her loneliness, her fatness, her boredom. All that was her responsibility now. She supposed it might be possible to do something about it, but it seemed a daunting challenge. She sat in her bedroom and looked at her round, plump face in the mirror and wondered how long it would take her to be thin. Then she went down to the kitchen and poured herself a glass of milk and took a handful of biscuits from the tin in the larder. Mrs Oliver was not there. Her father had said she would be in later but for the moment Fanny was deprived even of the distraction of an argument with her old adversary. After the usual bustle of the hotel – the noise and banter of the staff in the kitchen, the arrival and departure of guests the house seemed altered. Everyone moved more quietly and more slowly. The life had gone out of it and Fanny knew it would never be the same again.

She wandered back to her bedroom, switched on the television, then switched it off again. Nothing could entertain her. In the end she took *Animal Farm*, one of her school set texts, and sat in the window seat to read. She read in fits and starts, breaking off sometimes in mid sentence and wiping the condensation from the glass, to stare out of the window in listless contemplation.

It was some time later that she saw Mrs Oliver. The woman left the house by the kitchen door and set off down the path towards the walled vegetable garden. There was nothing unusual in that. Mrs Oliver often went out to empty the waste bin on the compost heap or to fetch vegetables for the kitchen, but there was something about her which caught Fanny's attention. She looked peculiar of course, but she always did. She was wearing enormous black

wellingtons which Fanny had never seen before and her awful
brown coat that looked like a dressing gown. In one hand she
carried two carriers bags and in the other a basket. Fanny recognized
the basket as her mother's. Its contents were covered by a checked
tea towel.

For a moment it occurred to Fanny to run downstairs to follow
Nan Oliver and see where she was going. The idea of this action
lifted her depression, but it was cold and wet outside and she did
not want the bother of changing her shoes and putting on a coat.
It was too much like hard work. Nan Oliver was probably on
some boring if eccentric chore for her mother. Besides, it was nearly
lunch time. She fetched a chocolate peppermint bar from a drawer
in her dressing table. With a sigh she settled back to *Animal Farm*,
but the sight of Mrs Oliver flapping up the path in wellingtons
three sizes too big for her had amused her and she had lost the
dreadful sense of foreboding and emptiness.

They all had lunch together in the kitchen, even Nan Oliver and
the peculiar old lady whom Helen claimed was a private detective.
Fanny could not imagine anything less like a private detective.
Helen had gone out and said she might not be back for lunch, so
they had started without her. Fanny could tell that her father was
not very pleased. Perhaps he knew about Laurie Oliver and
disapproved of him too. It was good, she thought, that Helen was
in trouble for once. It was just a shame Eleanor wasn't there to
see it too. Fanny had become sick of her grandmother saying
complimentary things about Helen.

There was home-made vegetable soup for lunch, which Fanny
ate although she did not enjoy it much. She preferred the stuff out
of a tin. But afterwards there was one of Mrs Oliver's chocolate
cakes, which were always delicious.

As Mrs Oliver got up to clear the soup plates Fanny noticed
that her feet were soaking wet. Her stockings were so wet that
there was a dark tide mark which reached almost to her knees.
But she was wearing wellingtons Fanny thought, and giggled at
the memory. She was going to ask the woman where she had been

going, but her mother handed her a large slice of chocolate cake and she forgot all about it.

No one said very much at lunch, except Veronica whose chatter was so persistent and inane that no one took any notice of it. There was a story about the flowers in the church on Easter Sunday which Fanny had heard several times before. Only her father pretended to be interested in it. And Molly Palmer-Jones. She seemed to be interested in everything. Because Nan Oliver had been late to work and because the whole routine of the house had fallen apart after Eleanor's death, it had been a late lunch. It had been almost two o'clock when they sat down and by the time the plates were cleared and they were sitting over the dregs of the coffee it was almost three.

'We might as well make the most of this,' Veronica said. 'We'll have more guests next week.'

'Are you sure,' Richard said, 'that you want people in so soon? We can always put them off.'

'No,' Veronica said. 'With any luck it will all be over by then. They'll surely catch the man soon.'

Then, aware of a lack of tact she blushed and looked at Nan Oliver who had begun to stack plates in the dishwasher. But the woman seemed not to have heard and continued the work without pause. Only Molly was aware of a stiffness of her neck and a tightening of her grip on the handle of the dishwasher door.

They had all finished and were reluctantly preparing to leave the warmth of the kitchen. It was bright and cheerful there and they were enjoying the companionship which they missed in the rest of the house. Suddenly Helen burst in. She was wearing a bright blue jacket and her hair was covered in a mist of raindrops. She was breathless and excited.

'Have the police phoned yet?' she asked.

'No,' Richard Mead said sharply. He still seemed annoyed because she had not made the effort to be back for lunch. 'Why should they have done?'

Helen looked at Nan Oliver and spoke directly at her. 'They've found Steve,' she said. 'I went to see Laurie and the police came there. He was stopped at Dover by the customs.'

'Was he trying to leave the country?' Molly asked.

'No,' Helen said. 'He was trying to get back in. The police think he had smuggled the birds out and was on his way home. They're bringing him back to Sarne for questioning tonight.'

Chapter Ten

Pritchard had been told of Stephen Oliver's arrest while he and George were still at Puddleworth, and on the car journey to Gorse Hill George had to tolerate Pritchard's triumphant good humour. The policeman seemed convinced that the inquiry was all but over and that Stephen Oliver would lead them to his father. He sang snatches of Welsh hymns and even expected George to join in the mood of jubilation and self-congratulation.

'It was all your doing,' he said. 'If your wife hadn't found out about the passports, customs wouldn't have been so vigilant. They're usually a dozy lot, customs officers.' And he began to sing 'Cwm Rhondda' with joyous abandon, his head back; all trace of fatigue gone.

George found it hard to share Pritchard's optimism. There had been no real evidence to prove that Kerry Fenn had begun the agency to supply falconers with birds and eggs, or that she had developed it to its present sophistication. She seemed very young for such a responsibility. It seemed to him that for the past two days they had been misled, and that the trail took them back to Gorse Hill.

Pritchard took George straight back to Gorse Hill. He would have time to go home and spend part of the evening at least with Bethan and the boys, before young Oliver arrived from the south coast. He was in a hurry. He wanted to be back for bath time.

They arrived at the hotel at six o'clock and for the first time that day the rain had stopped. The house seemed ordinary, comforting. It seemed impossible to George then that violence had been planned there; Pritchard must be right after all. Eleanor's death had been caused by unhappy chance, not premeditation. George stepped out of the car to the smell of cedar and wet grass.

'Thank you,' he said, like a polite child who has been taken for a treat by an estranged parent. 'It was a very interesting couple of days.' He was tired and glad to be back. He wanted a hot bath and a drink, and to be left alone.

'I'll come and pick you up later,' Pritchard said, 'when I go to interview the boy.'

'Oh no,' George said. 'I couldn't impose on you any further.'

'No question of imposition,' Pritchard said. 'We're all on the same side.' He looked sharply at George. 'You do want to come?' he said. 'You do want to see the thing through?' Then answering his own question, 'Of course you do. You're a professional. You couldn't let it go now.'

'No,' George said. It was true. He could not give up now. 'I'll see you later then.' He walked stiffly over the gravel and up the steps into the house.

Molly heard the car on the drive and from their bedroom window saw her husband, walking as straight as an old soldier on a British Legion parade, enter the hotel. She was unaccountably nervous, as if she were about to meet a stranger. Her resentment over his inability to see Eleanor Masefield clearly, as the unpleasant, dictatorial woman she was, still irked her, yet she was very glad to see him home. She went into their bathroom and began to run a bath and put the towels on the radiator to heat, so when he found her she was standing in a cloud of steam, and her spectacles were misted so she could not see him.

'I thought you might like a bath,' she said, taking off her glasses and wiping them ineffectually with her cardigan.

Despite his tiredness he could tell something was wrong. She was usually completely natural, but now there was a constraint in her voice. She wanted to let him know that she was displeased with him and for some reason would not say so outright. How tedious it must have been for her here with nothing to do!

'I'm sorry I went,' he said, 'without properly asking you first.

You are my partner. I should have asked if you thought it would be worth it.'

'Was it worth it?' she asked and he thought she seemed happier and that he had said the right thing.

'I don't know,' he said. 'I'll tell you about it when I'm in the bath.'

'All right,' she said, 'but I've something to tell you first.' He lay back in the large old bath and she sat on a cork stool beside him. He was surprised that she took control of the conversation so readily. She told him first about the phone call she had taken from the man with the foreign accent. George was unexpectedly interested.

'Tell me exactly what the man said,' he demanded, but found it hard to be authoritative lying with water and bubbles up to his neck.

'He said that Kerry Fenn had suggested that he ring. He told me it was a business matter.'

Molly did not resent his imperious tone. It was a habit, she thought. He did not mean it.

'It did not occur to me at first,' she said, 'but then I thought that any link between the Fenns and Gorse Hill was important.'

'It is, of course,' he said. He climbed out of the bath and dressed.

'Tell me what you found out,' she said.

'It seems there is a thriving business operation – an agency supplying falconers with eggs and birds,' he said. 'Frank Oliver and a taxidermist called Theo Williams have systematically been taking birds and eggs from the wild. Kerry Fenn is involved in it too. Pritchard thinks she is the organizing influence. But it seems to me she is too young. I got the impression that the agency's been established for years. It runs very smoothly and they seem to have developed contacts all over the world. Kerry Fenn only left school three years ago. Even though her father is a well-known falconer, I doubt if she would be sufficiently trusted to provide birds for the class of customer the business seems to be supplying.'

'So you think someone else might be involved?' she asked.

'Yes,' George said.

'And the phone call would suggest it's someone at Gorse Hill?'

'Don't you think that's possible?' Again it seemed to George that he was dependent on Molly to form his opinions. I'm tired, he thought as he waited for her to answer. She considered.

'It would be a much more plausible motive for murder,' she said. 'I always found it hard to accept the explanation that Eleanor was killed because she had interrupted someone stealing the birds. She was close to whoever killed her.'

'You could be right,' he said. 'And then the body was arranged so dramatically.'

'Why do you think she was killed?' Molly asked. He felt for a moment patronized, as if she were consulting him as a matter of form. But when he looked at her he saw that she really wanted to know.

'I believe someone at Gorse Hill was behind the falconry agency. Eleanor found out so she had to be murdered.'

'Is that likely?' Molly said. 'If so, why would the murderer arrange her body so near the falcons? The police were bound then to make the falconry connection and find out about the agency.'

'I don't know,' George said. 'Really I don't know.'

'I think the falconry's a red herring,' Molly said flatly. 'I think Eleanor was killed because of the sort of woman she was.'

'Of course Pritchard's convinced Oliver's the murderer,' George said a little desperately, avoiding the implication of her last statement. 'We'll have to find some definite proof to persuade him otherwise.'

'You do realize,' she persisted, 'that none of her family liked her? Even Veronica is glad that she's dead. She manipulated them all.'

What's she doing to me? George thought. Why is she behaving like some idiotic newlywed who needs endless reassurances that she's loved? Why is it so important to her? For God's sake, she must know that I never had any intention of having a wild, passionate affair with Eleanor Masefield. I'm too old for that. So what does she want me to say? That I hated the woman too? She knows that's not true.

Then he saw how important it was to Molly that he should answer her unspoken question. She wanted to know what he had felt for Eleanor. She wanted to know if the memory of the woman would remain with them for ever, coming between them at times of crisis. Yet he found it hard to speak. They had lived together for so long and knew each other so well that there had been no reason, for many years, to have this sort of conversation.

'I'll trust your judgement about Eleanor Masefield,' he said. 'I was infatuated with her beauty. Now I don't think I knew her very well at all.' He hesitated. 'It was never anything important,' he said. 'It was never anything that really mattered.'

'No,' she said. 'I don't think it was.'

She kissed him and they went to join the family for dinner.

Richard had laid a table in the dining room and cooked a meal for them himself. Nan Oliver had disappeared when she heard the news of Stephen's arrest. George found them all calmer than they had been before he went to Puddleworth. They were a normal family again, more normal even than they had been when Eleanor was still alive. He understood then what Molly had been trying to tell him. In Eleanor's presence the family had found it impossible to be themselves. There had been a hectic attempt at deception in order to please her. Now Richard Mead brought bottles of wine to the table and it was almost as if the meal was a feast of celebration at Eleanor's disappearance.

It was Molly who mentioned Eleanor and then the family seemed a little annoyed as if she were guilty of bad manners.

'How will you manage at Gorse Hill without Eleanor?' she asked. 'It's hard to imagine the hotel without her. She was such a good organizer wasn't she? And she always seemed so much in control.'

'Richard's a brilliant organizer too,' Veronica said, looking around the table for support from the girls. 'He's always done most of the work.'

'Of course we'll miss Grandmother,' Helen said dismissively, 'but she had some very peculiar ideas, you know. She was so old-fashioned!'

Then George realized that the new gaiety was a sham too. They were pretending to be stronger than they were. What right had they to suggest that they had never needed Eleanor, that they had never been dependent on her? He wished that Molly had not spoilt the meal with her question. He knew she was emphasizing her theory that Eleanor's character was an important factor in the crime, but he was convinced that the falconry agency was involved in her murder too. She was not killed simply because she was a dominating, interfering old lady. He had regained sufficient confidence in his own judgement to be sure of that.

Pritchard was later than George had expected and he thought perhaps the policeman had changed his mind and decided to interview Stephen Oliver alone. He waited on the porch at the top of the stone steps for Pritchard to arrive, hoping the fresh air would clear his mind and make him less tired. There was no moon, but occasionally the breeze would separate the cloud and there would be a scatter of stars. A tawny owl called from the trees behind the house. He began to relax and to feel able to take control of the investigation once more.

He saw headlight beams through the trees and a car pulled up on the gravel.

Pritchard's mood had changed completely. At first George thought there may have been some private grief – perhaps one of his boys was ill or a relative had died – and he did not like to ask what was wrong. Pritchard sat still and made no move to drive away or to talk to George. He seemed absorbed in some sadness or guilt of his own. He might have been drunk. Outside the car the wind blew through the trees and the owl called again.

'It something the matter?' George asked at last. He felt foolish sitting there in the dark. Perhaps Pritchard would release him now, let him go back to Gorse Hill where he had more important things to think of.

'We were wrong all the time,' Pritchard said. He was feeling not grief, but anger at his own incompetence. His pride had been hurt.

'In what way? Have you spoken to the boy?'

'Yes,' Pritchard said. 'Briefly.' And he was silent again.

'Did he see his father kill Eleanor Masefield?' Impatience was leading to irritation.

'He says, he didn't see Eleanor Masefield at all,' Pritchard said, 'and I believe him. He's frightened. If he knew anything about the murder he would have said so. Frank Oliver was with him all that Sunday afternoon. The whole trip to Puddleworth and Wolverhampton was a waste of time.'

'No,' George said. 'Not quite that, I think.' And he explained that he thought someone at Gorse Hill was organizing the thefts. 'Both Frank Oliver and Kerry Fenn had the hotel's phone number,' he said, 'and while we were away my wife took a phone call from someone who said he had been recommended to the place by Kerry Fenn and he wished to discuss a business matter. Don't you think it's possible that Eleanor Masefield found out that the racket was organized from Gorse Hill, demanded to see the culprit and was killed when she threatened to make the thing public, if it wasn't stopped?'

'Yes,' Pritchard said. 'I suppose that's possible. If you're right we only have to discover who was organizing the theft and sale of the birds and we have the murderer. The boy might have some idea who was employing him. Come with me and we'll talk to him again. I'd like your opinion of him. Frank Oliver will certainly know who was running the agency, so it's still a priority to find him.'

His mood of self-pity forgotten, he pushed the car into gear and drove fast down the drive.

The police station was Victorian red brick, built near the cattle market next to the magistrates' court. Mrs Oliver was sitting on a bench in the gloomy waiting area near the desk. She sat crouched with fatigue, her back round, her elbows on her knees, fat as a toad. As they came in she looked at them with hatred, as though she would like to spit at them. Yet George thought too that he saw triumph in her eyes as if she sensed the investigation had gone wrong for the police and that soon they would have to let her son go.

'Have you seen Stephen?' Pritchard asked. He felt sorry for her. He was used to being disliked and took no notice of her hostility.

She nodded towards the desk sergeant. 'He let me speak to him through the cell door,' she said. She felt no gratitude for the favour.

'Would you like me to arrange a lift home for you?'

'No,' she said. 'I'll wait for him.'

'You could have a long wait.'

'All the same I'll stay,' she said. 'You can take us both home when you've finished.'

She seemed quite confident that Stephen would be released.

Pritchard arranged for the boy to be brought into an interview room. He was as small and dark as his father, his hair cut like all the other youths of his age. His clothes which he had probably once thought smart were dirty and crumpled. He seemed weak and frightened and very tired. The customs officer had said he had been in a poor state when they found him. It had been a rough crossing and he had been sick all the way across the Channel. Perhaps in this small town on his home territory he could be cocky and arrogant – he would know all the angles – but tonight there was no sign of that jaunty, bullying self-confidence. Beside Pritchard's massive bulk he seemed a child.

Pritchard sat opposite the boy and shook his head sadly.

'You're in trouble, lad,' he said, fatherly and concerned. 'I don't know what's going to happen to you.'

'I didn't know about the old lady,' the boy said, his eyes wide with the effort of convincing them. Pritchard assumed the expression of one who has heard it all before. 'I didn't know she was dead until I saw a newspaper on the boat coming home. I couldn't believe it when it said the police were looking for Dad.'

'So why did you run away?' Pritchard asked.

'I didn't run away,' the boy said, bewildered. 'I was doing a job for my father.'

'I think,' Pritchard said gently, 'you'd better tell me all about it again.'

'He needed a messenger,' the boy said proudly, 'to take something to the continent. He knew I needed the money so he asked me.'

'Was that all he asked you to do?'

'No,' Stephen said. He still seemed unsure how much to say. He had promised his father he would keep quiet and although he had already told Pritchard everything, the words seemed a kind of betrayal.

'You helped him to steal some peregrines?'

The boy nodded. 'They were only birds,' he said. 'What's all the fuss about?' There was a trace of the old cockiness.

'Tell me what happened.'

'Dad went down the rope,' Stephen said. 'I'm no good at that sort of thing. I stayed at the top and kept a lookout. Two old ladies came up the lane and walked right past us but they thought we were rock climbing. Dad was really cool. When he got back up the cliff he stopped and chatted to them, and the chicks were in his rucksack all the time.'

'When did you take the birds?' Pritchard asked.

'On Sunday afternoon,' Stephen said. 'Dad helped Mr Fenn with the display and then met me by the barn. Mr Fenn was expecting him back to put the birds away, but Dad said it wouldn't hurt him to do it by himself for once.'

'Was he in his blue van?'

'Yes. He'd parked it by the barn earlier that afternoon. It was hidden by the building so you couldn't see it from the lane. He'd told Fenn the tax was out of date and he didn't want to leave it at the hotel.'

'What happened when your father had brought up the peregrines from the eyrie?'

'We got off the hill as soon as we could get rid of the old ladies. The adult birds were going wild, making a terrible noise. The ladies didn't seem to notice but the noise really got on my nerves. I wanted to get away from there.'

'What did you do with the birds?' George asked quietly.

'Dad looked after them. He had a special box for them. I didn't have anything to do with them until I got to Dover. The woman looked after them until then.'

'What woman?'

'The woman who drove me to Dover. When we got there we wrapped the box in pretty paper to make it look like a present. No one asked me about it when we went through customs.'

'Where did you meet the woman?'

'At Shrewsbury station. She was going to come with me all the way to France, but something seemed to have gone wrong. She and Dad talked at the station. I couldn't hear what they were saying. Dad seemed to want to call the whole thing off, but she said we ought to go ahead anyway. I suppose she'd heard that the old lady had been killed.'

'What was the woman's name?' Pritchard demanded. But if he were hoping to discover the Gorse Hill connection he was disappointed.

'Dad called her Kerry,' Stephen said. 'I don't know her other name. She wasn't much older than me.'

'Did your father go with you to Dover?'

Stephen shook his head. 'We left him at Shrewsbury,' he said. 'I don't know what he did then. I thought he must be going to Wolverhampton.' He paused. 'I was going to go and live with him,' he said, 'when I got back. He said there'd be more chance of a job in the town and I could work for him again, perhaps do other trips to Europe.'

'Why didn't you tell your mother where you were going?' Pritchard asked sternly. 'She's been worried about you.'

'Dad told me not to. Anyway I thought I'd only be away a couple of days and she's used to me going off for weekends with my mates. She was only worried because of what happened to the old lady;' He was beginning to regain some of his old disagreeable nonchalance. 'She knows I can look after myself.'

'What happened when you got to Calais? Did someone meet you?'

'Someone was supposed to meet me at the railway station on the Monday evening,' he said. 'I hung around all day. Dad had given me some food for the birds and I looked after them just like he told me. I wanted to do everything right.'

They could imagine him in the foreign land, lonely and unsure of himself, wandering around the unfamiliar streets, carrying his peculiar parcel. Perhaps he had drunk too much on the boat to boost his confidence and was feeling ill. He had never been abroad before. Stephen continued his story:

'I got to the station in plenty of time and waited in the café, which was just as Dad described it.'

'What was the person like?' Pritchard asked. 'Was he English?'

Stephen Oliver shook his head. 'No one came,' he said simply. 'I didn't know what to do. I waited for hours until the café shut.'

'Where did you stay?'

'With some English people,' Stephen said, 'who had a small hotel. Dad had fixed it up. I think he had stayed there before.'

Pritchard became excited by this, demanded details, the address, the names of the owners, but George thought it was unlikely now that Frank Oliver had left the country.

'I didn't know what to do then,' Stephen said. 'I was supposed to take the ferry back the next day. I didn't have much money. Dad had given me some, but I didn't have a lot to spare. I still had the birds. I thought perhaps there was some mistake and the bloke would turn up the next day. I was really knackered but I went back to the station that evening.'

'Did the falconer turn up?'

'No,' Stephen said. 'I was getting desperate. I thought I'd cocked the whole thing up. So I decided to come home.'

'Did you have no means of contacting your father in an emergency?' George asked.

The boy shook his head. 'No,' he said. 'Dad said there would be no problem. If my contact couldn't meet me at the station he would get in touch with me at the hotel. But there was no message, no phone call. I just wanted to get home. Then on the ferry I saw the newspaper and realized the police were looking for Dad.'

'What did you do with the chicks?' Pritchard asked.

'I threw them away,' he said. 'I was sick of the whole thing. I threw them into the sea.'

They sat in silence. Outside a drunk was being brought into the station. They could hear him shouting and swearing at the desk sergeant.

'When you were on the hill,' George said, 'did you hear anything unusual?'

'Dad thought his van was being nicked,' the boy said, with a sudden return of memory. 'He'd left his keys in it and he thought he heard it being driven down the lane. But when we got back it was still there.'

'You didn't see anyone?'

'Only the old ladies on the hill.'

The drunk in the corridor launched into a rousing version of Onward Christian Soldiers'.

'Where's your father, Stephen?' Pritchard asked. 'Just tell us and you can go home.'

'How should I know?'

'Did he get in touch with you in Calais? Is that why you spent so long in France?'

'No,' Stephen insisted, angry and frightened. 'I told you what happened. I haven't heard from him since we dropped him in Shrewsbury on Sunday.'

'Why would your father want to murder Eleanor Masefield?' Pritchard asked.

'He wouldn't want to murder anybody,' Stephen said. 'He was happy. He said he had a good business. He enjoyed working at Puddleworth and making a little bit on the side. He wouldn't do anything to upset all that.'

The point was so obvious and so logical that there was little they could say. George could sense Pritchard's defeat and asked one last question, knowing as he asked it that he was unlikely to receive an answer.

'Did your father tell you who they were all working for?' he asked. 'Did he say who organized his business?' But the boy shook his head. He was exhausted. There was nothing more he could tell them.

They let him go then. There was no reason to hold him. He would be charged with theft of the peregrines and with taking them illegally out of the country. He would appear in a magistrates' court, plead guilty and be fined. George doubted if he would pay the fine himself. It would be paid, like his other expenses, by his father's employer.

They all left the interview room together. Mrs Oliver was still on the bench, motionless, kept awake by her anger. Pritchard sat beside her and spoke confidentially to her as if they were alone.

'You're lucky,' he said. 'We're letting your son come home to you. If you know where Frank is, tell him we want to talk to him. We don't think he killed Mrs Masefield, not any more. But we think he may be in danger. We can give him the protection he needs.'

She stood up stiffly to be beside her son. She ignored Pritchard and though she said nothing they could tell she did not believe him.

Chapter Eleven

George fell asleep quickly and slept deeply, but woke very early in the morning. It was just getting light and there was a clear burst of bird song from the trees outside the window. Molly was still sleeping. She lay on her back with her arms outstretched, palms up, fingers curled in relaxation.

He trusted Molly's judgement about Eleanor Masefield. How could I have been so wrong about her? he thought. He had seen her as the charming, beloved matriarch, devotedly keeping her business and the weaker members of the family together. Now it seemed they would be happier without her. Does it matter that I was wrong about her? he thought. I found her compelling, beautiful. Do I really care that she was insensitive to her family's needs? It was what she thought of me that counted and I'll never know that now.

He got out of bed and dressed without disturbing Molly, then went downstairs. There was a cold, grey light and a gusting wind which rattled round the chimneys. Inside everywhere was quiet. The office door was unlocked and he went in. He told himself that he was looking for evidence that someone at Gorse Hill was involved with stealing and selling falcons but that was not entirely true. He was hoping to find some relic of Eleanor, a letter, a photograph, a diary, which would justify his infatuation for her, which would re-create her as the woman he had known. The fact that the office door was unlocked led him to suppose that he had little chance of finding anything incriminating. Besides, it had been Eleanor's place. She would have come across any records or accounts for the sale of birds which might be hidden there. But because it had been Eleanor's place he went in and began to look around.

The room was still dark, because it faced on to the hill, so he had to switch on an electric light. It was more functional than it had been in Stuart Masefield's day. The photographs of birds of prey remained on the walls, the shelves of dusty, leatherbound books were still there, but the stuffed birds and the eggs had gone. He wondered if Eleanor kept the books and the photographs in memory of Stuart or if she used them like wallpaper to give colour and warmth to the room. The shotguns, with which Stuart had played country gentleman with Theo Williams' father, were still in the room, but put away discreetly in a wall cupboard.

On a desk near the window was a computer keyboard and visual display unit. Eleanor had called it 'Richard's toy'. He used it to keep a check on bookings, to make up the accounts and to send confirmation to prospective customers. For a moment George was excited. Surely a computer would be useful in matching requests for falcons with information of known sites. Only Richard Mead knew how to use the computer. No one else had access to it. It would be an ideal way of keeping the Falconry Centre secret. George looked at the machine warily. He had no idea how to make it work. There would surely be some codework to release the information on the agency but he dared not touch the computer. Then he realized that the idea of Richard Mead as head of an aggressive illegal business was ridiculous. Meek, mild-mannered Mead would not know where to begin. George was still confident enough in his own judgement to see that.

The other desk was Eleanor's. He could remember it in the room when it had been Masefield's study. George looked quickly through the drawers. The contents were jumbled and untidy as if someone had been looking there before him in a hurry. The police would have looked, but they would have been more orderly in their search. There was nothing of interest in the drawer except a copy of Eleanor's will, which left Gorse Hill and everything else she owned to Veronica. That was as expected. He supposed the police would have been in touch with Eleanor's solicitor already and would have seen the original.

He was about to close the drawer when he found a crumpled black and white photograph, stuck between the drawer and the back of the desk. It was of Eleanor in an evening dress. It had been taken, he guessed, just before the war. She was very young. He imagined again the grand parties there might have been at Gorse Hill, thought of women's laughter on the frosty air, music and voices. I was in love with a dream, he thought, with a young man's idea of glamour. He turned the photograph over. On the back was written: 'To Stuart with all my love. Eleanor'. He took one last look at the picture of the girl then replaced it in the desk. She was beautiful, he thought. I was right, at least, about that.

He had found what he wanted and was ready to leave the room and return to bed, but he was drawn to the books. Stuart had a strange collection, he thought. All the expected works were there – Leslie Brown's *British Birds of Prey* and Radcliffe's book on the peregrine – but a complete set of the *New Naturalist* series stood next to a row of *Beano* annuals. The books seemed to be arranged according to size and visual appearance rather than subject matter. On the bottom shelf was a series of heavy, thick books, too big to fit elsewhere. There was a family bible, the memoirs of a Victorian egg collector with illustrations and diagrams and a glossy coffee-table book on heraldry and coats of arms. Next to it was a book with a similar binding to the bible, but with no title on the spine. George carefully pulled it out. As he lifted it off the shelf and on to the desk there was surprisingly little dust. He opened the pages and found that it was not a printed book at all, but an old-fashioned ledger, with a wide margin and fine, narrow lines. Stuart Masefield had used it as a diary.

The entries began in the late fifties and at first they were sketchy, with perhaps just one or two dates listed in a year. They were concerned with his search for raptors' nest sites. The language Masefield used in the diary was exaggerated and dated and he seemed eager to portray himself as a naturalist in the Victorian tradition, but despite the falsely archaic phrasing his triumph and passion came through. He had found a golden eagle nest in the Cairngorms which was easily accessible. At the end of the summer he had walked into the eyrie and smoked a pipe there. His excitement had a feverish, childlike quality.

From the later entries in the diary it became clear that his friends in the falconry world began to prey on his vanity, and suggested that he prove his skill at nest-finding by providing them with eggs and young. George thought that the device of seeing the theft as a test or challenge of his competence could not have deceived Stuart Masefield. He was obviously unbalanced, but not a fool. He had enjoyed plundering the nests. It had given him a sense of power over the natural world, and soon it became obvious that he saw the financial potential of his actions. In the early 1970s he sold two young peregrine falcons to 'an arab buyer' for £500 plus expenses. In the years before his death his activities appeared to become more organized and there was the first record of his having employed an assistant. He was stealing a clutch of eggs from a goshawk nest and wrote: 'Sent Frank Oliver up the tree. I'm not sufficiently agile for that sort of thing now'. Soon after there was a reference to Theo Williams: 'Theo has become indispensable. His ability to find breeding birds is astounding. I wonder now how I ever managed without him'.

George had expected the diary to end with Masefield's death, but it was continued almost immediately in a different handwriting, in a handwriting which George recognized, because he had seen it that morning on the back of a photograph. The realization that Eleanor Masefield was running the agency was less shocking than it would have been before he had begun to read the diary. She and Stuart were close, allies and partners. It seemed only natural that she should succeed him. After her husband's death it seemed she had been determined to continue his unofficial business and to bring to it her own ruthlessness and organizational skill. It was quite clear from the records in the diary that she was in charge of the enterprise. All the accounts were kept in the book and George was astonished by the scale of the operation and the sums of money she made each year. She imported illegal birds as well as exporting them. It was no wonder, he thought, that she had afforded an expensive car and could keep Gorse Hill so well. While Stuart had made a little extra pocket money from his adventures, Eleanor Masefield's income was considerably boosted by the agency.

In her elegant, sloping handwriting Eleanor went on to record how Kerry Fenn had been recruited as a glorified secretary and to liaise with the foreign customers. She went abroad for her father and could always find an excuse for an extra visit. She did all the agency's typing at home, but seemed to have little responsibility. It had been relatively easy, Eleanor wrote, to persuade Kerry to join the team. Lydia Fenn had been a wealthy woman and after her accident Murdoch Fenn had built Puddleworth with her money. But that had all gone and the running costs of the Centre had nearly outstripped income. The money Kerry made by working for Eleanor at least contributed to the expenses of Murdoch's beloved Falconry Centre. Eleanor had exploited Kerry's affection for her father and his dependence on the place for his happiness.

Later, some months before her murder, Eleanor had considered the question of the Sarne peregrines.

'While I'm reluctant to disturb the Sarne falcons – after all they were Stuart's favourites,' she had written, 'I feel it would be foolish to turn down such a lucrative offer'. There followed details of the financial terms offered by a German businessman. The moral deliberations were soon over and she had concluded: 'So long as no suspicion falls on Gorse Hill I can see nothing against it.'

Then she had made every effort to present herself as a champion of the peregrines, insisting that the birds should be protected, knowing all the time that none of the conservation groups would agree to her demands. The town must be persuaded, when the birds were taken, that she had been right all the time.

A week before her death there was an indication that someone was close to discovering her secret. 'Impossible to stop Sarne operation now,' she wrote. 'Must take every step to throw suspicion elsewhere'.

And then there had been frantic efforts to persuade the family that a blue van was haunting the lane and that the birds were in danger. When the peregrines disappeared everyone would then believe that the mysterious man in the blue van had taken them. Even if, by some extreme misfortune, Oliver was arrested, he would receive a minimal fine which she would pay and there would be nothing to connect him with her. The business would thrive, and the Sarne birds could be taken the following year. The important thing was to protect herself.

So George had been summoned. George, who was blinded by his infatuation and would take her part against the world. Of course she had refused to give him details of her concern. She wanted him there, to prove to whoever in Sarne had become suspicious about her activities that she wanted to protect the Gorse Hill birds in memory of Stuart. She did not want him to question her about the birds. So she had put him off, pretending to be too busy with the Open Day.

She used me, he thought, as she used everyone else. Molly was right and I was too arrogant to see it. He found it impossible to feel anger towards Eleanor. Her beauty had given him pleasure and had moved him just as the peregrines on the hill had given him pleasure. The fault was all his. He had deluded himself that she could find him attractive. She was ruthless and greedy and he had only cared what she thought about himself.

Then who killed her? he thought. Why would anyone want to see her dead? Because he had been so wrong about Eleanor he felt suddenly insecure about everything. His confidence deserted him. There were footsteps on the stairs outside the study door and he felt himself shaking. He thought he had never been so frightened. He did not know who had murdered Eleanor and he imagined each of the household, in turn, transformed into a grotesque killer. He held his breath, expecting the door to be opened, so that he would be confronted by the murderer, but the footsteps passed. When he had struggled to regain control, he felt a mixture of relief and shame, and then began to laugh, a little hysterically at his foolishness.

Fanny woke unusually early too. A day of boredom stretched ahead of her. It was unfair, she thought. Surely her grandmother's death should have brought some excitement – there should have been television cameras, handsome detectives, newspaper reporters. Instead she was trapped at Gorse Hill, sheltered by her parents from all the fuss. There had been policemen of course, but they had been boring, predominantly middle-aged, and had talked to her as if she were a child.

She turned over and settled under the duvet, but sleep was impossible. She had done so little, the day before, that she was not tired. At last, out of desperation, she got up.

I could do exercises, she thought, remembering her pledge to lose some weight. I could go for a run. The motivation and enthusiasm carried her through dressing and a skimpy wash, and saw her down the stairs. But by the time she got into the garden she had decided that after all, a gentle walk would suit her mood better. She remembered quite vividly the comical picture of Nan Oliver in oversized wellingtons, bent with the weight of basket and carrier bags. She would follow Mrs Oliver's trail down the garden. She would discover her secret.

She had no idea what she would find. The excitement was in being up early before the rest of the family, in the possibility of catching Nan Oliver at something of which her parents might disapprove, something which might make her appear ludicrous. She was still young enough to remember stories of witches – as a child it had been easy to imagine Nan Oliver as a witch – but she had no premonition of danger as she followed the path past the kitchen garden.

Although it had not rained during the night the grass was still damp and her footprints left marks on the path. I should have followed her yesterday, she thought. I'll never find out where she went now. Then she decided that the bags and the basket must be somewhere and it should be possible to find them. The path led between the red-brick wall of the kitchen garden and the flat grass lawn surrounded by sloping terraces where the folk singers had performed at the Open Day. Soon it would be mown and marked and turned into a tennis court for the guests. I'll have to take up tennis, she thought. That will keep my weight down. The sun was beginning to come up over the town and shone through the trees on to the red-brick wall and reflected on the greenhouse built against it.

It had been a long time since she had followed the path beyond the walled garden. When she and Helen were young it had been a treat to come to Gorse Hill on Sunday afternoon to explore the grounds. But it had been years since she had taken pleasure in that kind of activity. Beyond the tennis courts there was a strip of rhododendron thicket which had spread to surround a field, reached from the path by a five-barred gate. Eleanor usually let the field to a local farmer for his daughters' ponies – neither Helen nor Fanny had shown any interest in riding – but it had been empty all winter and the grass was long and mixed with cow parsley.

Beyond the field, in a small wood, there was a rookery and the black birds cawed and flapped above the tall trees. In one corner of the field was the old pigsty where Helen and Fanny had played so often. It had been Helen's secret place and Fanny only gained admission by learning special rites. She remembered that climbing to the top of the cedar tree had been one of the tasks to be achieved before entry became automatic. What a bossy cow Helen had been, she thought. No wonder she was such a favourite of Eleanor's.

At the gate she stopped. The game had lost its magic and she wondered at her madness at getting up so early and at her want of sophistication. What would the girls at school say if they could see her now? The long grass in the field would be very wet and she was ready for breakfast. But as she looked into the field she saw that the long grass had been trampled into a path between the gate and the pigsty. Someone had been there recently. Awkwardly she climbed the gate and walked along the new path towards the wood and the corrugated iron hut in the corner of the field. The grass on each side of her was nearly waist high. Still without any fear for her own safety, an innocent Goldilocks alone in the woods, she lifted the latch of the door and went inside.

'Did you guess that Eleanor was running the falconry agency?'

George asked. He was standing by the bedroom window. The room was at the front of the house and had no view of the kitchen garden or the rhododendron thicket.

'No,' Molly said. 'I never guessed that.' She was sitting up in bed drinking tea which Helen had brought for them. Her hair was as tousled as a small boy's. 'But of course it makes sense.'

'Do you know who killed her?' he asked. He wanted to tell her how frightened he had been in the study, but she answered with certainty before he had the opportunity.

'Yes,' she said. 'Now I know.' She told George who had murdered Eleanor Masefield, and why she was killed.

She could not tell how he reacted. His face was turned away from her as he stared out of the window. 'What should I do?' he said.

'Tell Pritchard to make an arrest before anyone else gets hurt.'

'Yes,' he said. 'I'll phone him now and ask him to come this morning.' He was quiet for a few moments then added: 'I suppose in a way that we were both right about the case.'

'I suppose we were,' she said. She got up and dressed and they walked arm in arm down the stairs for breakfast.

'I'll have to stay,' she said, 'for a couple of days. We can't just run away.'

He agreed with her though he wanted to run away more than anything else.

No one was surprised when Fanny failed to turn up for breakfast. She was lazy. She always overslept.

'Poor thing,' Veronica said. 'This business has upset her more than we've realized. Let her have a lie in. We can take her breakfast up on a tray later.'

But when Veronica carried the meal up to her younger daughter's bedroom and found it empty there was immediate concern. If she were awake it was out of character for Fanny to miss a meal. It was surprizing enough that she had got up before the rest of them, but she would certainly have been back for breakfast. Something must have happened to her. Veronica was frantic. She hurried to find Richard who wanted to telephone the police immediately. It was Molly, eventually, who persuaded them that it might be best to search for Fanny themselves first. She thought she knew why Fanny might be upset. She imagined her hidden, brooding and upset, and wanted to speak to her before the police arrived.

George asked Helen to go with him to search the hill. Richard and Veronica said they would look in the house and then in the front garden. Molly was left to do the kitchen garden, the tennis court and the paddock. She made it clear she preferred to be alone.

Molly followed the path the girl had taken earlier that morning, but she was thinking now not about Fanny but about George. She took no pleasure in having been the first to discover who had killed Eleanor Masefield. She had expected to feel triumphant because her way, the woman's way, of listening and understanding had succeeded when his had failed, but now she felt guilty because she had hurt his pride and destroyed his dream of the perfect woman. Why should I feel guilty? she thought. I've tolerated his superiority for years. We understand each other better now.

She had passed the walled garden and reached the rhododendron wood. There was no vegetation under the bushes. It was dark there and very quiet. She came out into the sunshine by the five-bar gate. She stopped and noticed, as Fanny had done, the path trampled through the grass. She saw the pigsty, surrounded by cow parsley and young nettles.

'Fanny!' she called. 'I want to talk to you. Fanny! Come out so I can explain what's going to happen.'

There was no reply. She climbed the gate, more nimbly than the girl had done, and began to cross the field.

'Fanny,' she said. 'I know you're there. I'm going to come in so we can talk about what happened.'

But Fanny did not appear. Instead there was the sound of a gunshot as Frank Oliver fired over Molly's head from the pigsty window.

'I've got the girl as hostage,' he shouted. Molly could not see his face. It was hidden by the shadow of the hut. 'If anyone comes any closer she's dead. I'm coming out and I'm bringing her with me.'

When Fanny had lifted the latch and stepped into the pigsty she had seen at first, caught in the sunlight shining like a spot light through the glassless window, two carrier bags, empty and folded, and on top of them a brown wicker basket. The tea towel had been removed from the basket and she could see half a loaf of bread, a pot of jam, cold meat, a couple of pieces of cooked chicken, cheese wrapped in cellophane and a banana. Mrs Oliver's gone loopy, she thought. Why should she want a picnic all by herself out here? Then she saw the wellingtons, standing by the wicker basket. In a dark corner something moved and a man swore and demanded to know who was there.

Frank Oliver was still lying in his sleeping bag, dressed only in shirt and underpants. She must have woken him. As her eyes became accustomed to the shadow she saw he was dirty and unshaven. She backed away from him and opened the door to run away.

'Stay where you are!' he said. He was the wolf of every fairy story and infant nightmare. 'I've got a gun. Now come in and sit on the floor where I can see you.'

She did as she was told and even in her terror she thought that nothing like this had ever happened to the other girls in her class and that they would have to listen to her now. The man got out of his sleeping bag and rested the shotgun on his knee while he dressed with one hand. Then he came out of the shadow and into the sunlight, so she could see his face clearly for the first time, and only then did she realize who he was, because he looked so like Laurie.

'You're Mrs Oliver's husband,' she said. 'The police say you killed my grandmother.' And there was no pleasure in her fear now. She was mindlessly, desperately frightened.

'Shut up,' he said. 'I want to think. Then you're going to help me get out of here.'

She was not wearing a watch and had no idea of time, but it seemed hours later when she heard Mrs Palmer-Jones calling her name. The man had been eating, still with one hand, still watching her like a hawk as he stuffed bread and meat into his mouth. She was too frightened to consider running away, too frightened even to feel hunger.

'Who's that?' he demanded as they heard Molly calling, looked through the window and saw her climb the gate.

'She was a guest at the hotel when my grandmother died,' Fanny said, 'and stayed on. Her husband was a friend of Eleanor's.'

She wondered if he would want to know that George Palmer-Jones was a private detective, but he motioned her to be quiet. He moved her roughly into the corner furthest away from the window, did something she did not see to the gun and fired it out of the window. She tried to scream but no sound came from her throat. She opened her mouth but the muscles at the back of her throat strained uselessly and there was still silence. She heard the man shouting out of the window. He can't have killed her, she thought. He wouldn't have been talking to her if he had killed her.

The man moved quickly away from the window and began to pack his sleeping bag, some clothes and the food into a small rucksack. He pulled on the big, black wellingtons.

'Stand up,' he shouted to her. 'You're going out first. Don't try to run away or I'll kill you. I've nothing to lose now.' He was talking to himself not to her, but she was almost hysterical and did not realize his desperation. 'Stand up,' he repeated. 'Walk out slowly into the field.' She could not realize that he was frightened too.

She scrambled to her feet and he pushed her out through the door. She was crying, but still made no noise. As he shoved her back she stumbled and he swore at her.

'Go on,' he shouted. 'Walk towards the gate.'

She went out into the bright sunlight. Molly was at the other end of the field, watching what was going on. Fanny knew the man was walking behind her, several yards away, the rucksack over his shoulder, holding the shotgun ready to fire. She longed to run towards the elderly lady, who was like a real grandmother, as kind and accepting as she had always imagined a grandmother to be.

'I'll want a car,' the man shouted to Molly. 'A fast car, full of petrol. I'll be taking the girl with me.'

'Let her go,' Molly said. 'The police know you didn't kill Eleanor Masefield.'

'You don't think I believe you,' he sneered. 'I'll be done for murder and one more body won't make any difference to what I get.'

'No,' Molly screamed. 'Don't be a fool.'

Then it seemed to Fanny that the woman was shouting not at Frank Oliver but beyond him. There was another sound of a gunshot behind her and she waited breathlessly for pain or death. The rooks, frightened again, rose in a cloud like bats.

'Fanny,' came the gentle, reassuring tone of her father's voice. 'It's all right now. It's all over.'

She turned and saw that Frank Oliver was lying on the field. His face was hidden by the long grass and nettles. He was still moving, still alive, holding his leg and groaning. She turned away from him again and ran into her father's arms. Still she found it impossible to speak.

She was confused by what happened next and the pain and confusion lasted for weeks. The kind old lady's husband appeared with the policeman. They walked through the grass up to her father. The old woman took Fanny gently into her arms. Then the policeman arrested her father and led him away.

Chapter Twelve

Pritchard insisted on buying George and Molly drinks that night, because the investigation was over and he wanted to celebrate. Now in the peace of the Hop Pole they discussed the events which had led to Mead's arrest and tried to make sense of them. The dim firelight and the pints of beer seemed to turn the facts of the case into a story, a television play they had watched together. They might have been discussing some scandal of the town which had happened years before. Yet the climax of the investigation had been reached that morning and was still vivid in all their minds.

The day had been fraught and chaotic and descended at times into farce. The first gunshots had brought them all running together towards the field, like children converging on an ice cream van. Richard Mead had arrived first, then George and Pritchard, because George had given up his idea of searching for Fanny on the hill when he had met Pritchard in the drive. He had wanted to bring the policeman up to date with his discoveries and share Molly's theory that Mead was the murderer. They reached the field in time to see Fanny walking from the pigsty, followed by Oliver; they heard Molly's cry and saw her waving her arms, stiffly, like a wind-crazed scarecrow. They heard the report of the shotgun, saw Oliver fall and the child run towards her father who emerged from the thicket of rhododendron to hold her to him. Only Molly had seen Richard Mead shoot Frank Oliver.

Mead had been in the house when he heard the first shot. He took Stuart Masefield's shotgun from the office and ran into the garden. Hidden by the bushes which circled the field he had watched Oliver and his daughter leave the pigsty. He had made his way through the rhododendrons until he was very close to Oliver. Molly saw him lift the gun and point it, then waver and aim not for the head but the leg. If Oliver had died it would be hard to prove Mead to be the murderer. Because the man was only injured Mead had ensured his own conviction. Molly had thought Fanny had run away because she guessed her father was the murderer and could not face up to the pain of it. Now her father had saved her and was an even greater hero to the girl.

When Oliver was shot George had hesitated. He thought the arrest could wait. Mead would not escape and there were more important things to do. The child had received enough of a shock already. But Pritchard wanted the thing over. Perhaps he thought it would be less painful now, while the girl was still hysterical and hardly knew what was happening. So the child had been prised from her father and Mead stood with quiet dignity while Pritchard formally charged him.

Then Veronica and Helen appeared, vengeful and angry, quite misinterpreting the situation. They thought Mead had been arrested because he had shot at Oliver and their indignation knew no bounds. They railed at Pritchard, attacking again and again like birds pecking at a carcass:

'You can't arrest my husband!'

'The man might have shot my sister!'

'He only did it to protect Fanny.'

'It was self-defence.'

Pritchard made a few attempts at tactful explanation then at last he shouted: 'Mr Mead killed Eleanor Masefield,' to protect himself against the women.

The wind was tearing at their shirts and their hair, turning them into pale, thin-faced monsters. They turned together to face Richard Mead.

'Is it true?' Helen demanded and there was something of her grandmother's arrogance in her posture and her certainty that she would be answered. Veronica, for the first time, was silent.

'Yes,' he said.

Veronica flinched as if she had been hit but did not cry or

crumple. She stood straight-backed, beside her daughter, facing the wind. In the trees behind the pigsty the birds cawed contentedly and fluttered back to their nests.

'Why did you do it?' Helen said.

'She would have destroyed you,' Richard Mead said. 'She would have destroyed us all.'

Into this confusion Nan Oliver and Laurie arrived, one fat and one thin, like a comic turn. Molly never found out quite how they came to be there. When she heard that Richard Mead had been arrested Mrs Oliver laughed. She had a loud raucous cackle like the call of the rooks. Then it seemed that the field was full of noise. There was the siren of an ambulance and the shouted obscenities of the injured man, Mrs Oliver's laughter and the straining engine of the police car which had tried to drive up the grass track to the field and got stuck in the mud.

Molly wrapped Fanny in her own coat, put her arm around her and walked her away from the folly of it all. Laurie walked gently towards Helen in an attempt to comfort her, but she turned away. To be pitied by him would be the final indignity.

Now Alan Pritchard, George and Molly sat in the Hop Pole, attended with great ceremony by Mary and Gertrude Cadwallader. It was late and Gertrude obviously saw great benefit in allowing Superintendent Pritchard to drink after hours. The curtains had been drawn so no one in the street could tell that business was still taking place. Gertrude had indicated her approval of the gathering by allowing a fire to be lit and by making them sandwiches without asking for payment.

'So it was Richard Mead all the time,' Pritchard said. He held a glass of beer. He was coherent, but even more cheerful, more inclined to enjoy himself than when he was perfectly sober. '. . . And I always thought he was such a pleasant kind of chap.'

'Have you spoken to Oliver?' George asked.

'I got a statement this afternoon,' Pritchard said. 'It would have saved a lot of trouble if he'd come forward at the beginning, of course, but he was scared stiff. He realized his van was used to move the body.'

'Why did Mead have to move her?' Molly asked.

'He was disturbed. The two old ladies Stephen Oliver saw on the hill walked up the lane. Mead had to do something quickly or they would have seen the body. The van was there with the keys inside. He couldn't go too far – he wanted to return the van before it was missed – so he drove to the back of Gorse Hill. Fenn was in his Range-Rover fast asleep. There was no one in the field and it was hidden from the rest of the proceedings of the Open Day so he was able to tip the body into the weathering ground without being seen.'

'Perhaps he got some satisfaction from that,' Molly said. 'Putting her body near to the birds of prey.'

Pritchard ignored the interruption and continued his story.

'No one missed Richard Mead,' he said. 'He was shut in the office for most of the afternoon. If anyone did go in and find the room empty, they would have assumed he was out in the garden helping.'

'So Oliver didn't suspect anything?' Molly said.

'Not until he got to Shrewsbury and met Kerry Fenn,' said George. 'Her father had phoned her by then and told her that Eleanor was dead. He probably told her too that Oliver was wanted for questioning. Oliver wanted to call off his son's trip to Europe but Kerry persuaded him that it should go ahead. She was ambitious. She thought she could carry on the business. But of course the European contact heard about Eleanor's murder too and was too scared to turn up.'

'Oliver said he thought if he stayed in hiding for long enough we would eventually find some detail which would prove he was innocent,' Pritchard said. 'Of course he's not very bright. He went to Theo Williams to ask for shelter and then when we were waiting for him at Farthing Ridge, he stole a shotgun from Williams' car.' He lifted himself out of his chair and went to the bar to order another round of drinks.

'It's hardly surprising that Richard seemed so devastated the day after Eleanor's murder,' Molly said when the policeman had returned. 'I thought he was just worried about Veronica and the girls. Veronica had realized that there was some tension between Richard and Eleanor. That's why she was so hysterical when Eleanor died – she suspected then that her husband was involved – so she was very relieved when I told her that Frank Oliver was the suspect.'

'I don't understand why he killed the old lady,' Pritchard said easily. 'He never seemed the violent type to me.'

'He wasn't,' Molly said. 'Not usually. But he's weak and he could find no other way to fight Eleanor Masefield's influence. Did George tell you that she was organizing the falconry agency?'

Pritchard nodded and they had to wait for him to empty his glass before the conversation could continue.

'Stuart Masefield began it all,' George said, 'but it was a game to him. He liked birds of prey, he liked handling them and photographing them. He enjoyed feeling he had power over them. So he took them from the wild. He was a little mad, I think. He didn't make a lot of money out of the thefts but made enough to allow him to be more selective about the sort of research he chose to do. Veronica told Molly that she wondered sometimes how the family survived financially. I think Stuart Masefield would take a clutch of peregrine eggs whenever a hefty bill arrived. The Puddleworth connection began with him too. He knew Murdoch Fenn very well and he went shooting with Theo Williams' father and his employer. Williams mounted some of the specimens which were in Stuart's study when we first visited, though Eleanor was sufficiently discreet to give all those away.

'Eleanor must have known about Masefield's hobby but she probably indulged him in it. She treated everyone around her as if they were children. Perhaps that's why she's not still alive. She was fond of her husband in her own way. She probably understood his fascination with the natural world. She too was of a class and a generation which saw all forms of wildlife as a means of amusing, diverting or feeding man.

'Then Stuart died and she decided to turn Gorse Hill into a hotel. She persuaded Veronica and Richard to come to live with her, not I think because she believed Veronica would be happier there, as she led us all to suppose, but to provide a cheap form of labour. The business was never fairly organized, Eleanor remained in control and the Meads were dependent on her for everything as if they were paid staff.'

'So Mead murdered her for money,' Pritchard interrupted. That was a motive he could understand. It was better than birds and family neuroses. Money was a motive which a court would understand. 'He should have had more patience. She was quite an old lady. She wouldn't have gone on for ever. The business would have come to Veronica Mead eventually.'

'I really don't think he murdered her for money,' Molly said, 'though it must have been an exciting prospect to be in charge of his own company again. He was doing most of the work after all and Eleanor gave him little credit for his contribution to the hotel.'

'Then why did he kill her?' Pritchard demanded. 'Most men hate their mothers-in-law. Mine is a real dragon and she costs me a fortune in phone bills. But I wouldn't kill her.'

'It was because of the falconry agency,' George said. 'When Stuart died Eleanor didn't have a lot of money. Stuart was feckless, irresponsible as she had enouraged him to be. He had made no provision for her future. She hoped the hotel would make a profit eventually, but at the beginning it must have been hard to make ends meet. As I've said she knew that Stuart was selling birds, though I don't think she realized how much money it was possible to make. We'll never know when she decided to turn the thing into an organized business. Perhaps she found Stuart's diary as I did and was stimulated by that or perhaps one of Stuart's foreign customers contacted Gorse Hill to ask for birds, not realizing he was dead.'

'This is all very interesting,' Pritchard said, now sounding quite aggressively and impatiently drunk, 'but will someone tell me exactly why Richard Mead killed Eleanor Masefield.'

'George told you,' Molly said, becoming impatient herself because he seemed so deliberately obtuse. 'It was because of the falconry agency. Once I knew Eleanor was in charge of it the thing became obvious.'

'Well it's not obvious to me,' Pritchard said sulkily. 'But I'm only a detective superintendent. . .'

'He loves his wife and children,' Molly said. 'That was clear from the start. He had no security himself as a boy – his father went bankrupt – and he was determined to look after them. It had become a kind of obsession with him. He had given up his independence and his own career to make Veronica happy and he wanted the best for the girls. He found out what Eleanor was doing and he saw it as a threat to everything he had worked for. I think she may have been careless about leaving files and accounts in her office and he must have realized that the business had substantial alternative sources of income. George thought someone had been through the drawers of her desk. Richard confronted her with it but she refused to stop stealing birds and eggs from the wild. He might have found it possible to live with that, but then it became obvious that she would try to involve Helen in the agency. That, I think, was the real motive for the murder. You must understand that Richard and Veronica thought Eleanor had unlimited influence. Because she dominated them they thought she would dominate the girls. Richard Mead must have had terrible visions of his daughters being led into crime by Eleanor and there being nothing he could do to stop it.'

'He could have told the police.'

'Then there would have been the court case with all the resulting publicity. He had a horror of that. He had been through a similar experience with his father's bankruptcy. And he didn't want Veronica to know. She's always been easily depressed and he was afraid of making her ill. Besides, if Eleanor were found guilty and received substantial fines for all the birds taken, the money would have come out of the business and the family would lose in the end.'

Back to money, Pritchard thought with satisfaction. Back to a real motive. But the beer had made him charitable and after all the old lady had speeded up the investigation through her own brand of psychology, so he did not mention the point. He remembered the quiet, formal interview he had had with Mead that afternoon.

'He arranged to meet Mrs Masefield on the hill,' Pritchard said, 'to make one last attempt to stop her and to persuade her to leave his daughter alone. She laughed at him. He told me that this afternoon. She laughed at him and said that someone had to provide for his family and give them a future. He was no good to them. She said he wouldn't have the nerve to tell the police what she was doing. Helen was the only one in the family with any guts. Mead said he never went to the hill intending to kill her. There was a loose boulder, part of the drystone wall. He picked it up and hit her head with it. Perhaps he'll get away with manslaughter. He'll come over well in the witness box.' And then, speaking almost to himself, he added: 'I don't suppose it matters why he killed her. He's confessed. We don't need any more than that.'

The investigation was over. It was a time for celebration. He lifted his glass to them.

George and Molly left Gorse Hill early the next morning but the three women were up to see them off. Molly had been astonished by their realism and their strength. They would wait for Richard and support each other until he came home. If they needed to sell Gorse Hill to survive they would do that too. As George and Molly packed their bags into the car the Meads stood in a line on the steps, upright and undefeated, like women portrayed in Soviet propaganda art looking forward to a hard but honourable future. Perhaps when they were alone they cried, but there was no sign of that now. They did not speak.

George thought that perhaps he would come back and stay at Gorse Hill, but it would never be the same. Gorse Hill had represented all the joy and colour in his childhood. Nowhere else at Sarne meant so much to him. The remembered dream of taking a young Eleanor into his arms and dancing with her over the frosty grass had lost all its significance. The magic had gone, and with it the attraction of coming home.

Molly started the engine and began to drive slowly away from the house. When George turned to wave goodbye to the Meads they had gone, quite suddenly, and the steps were empty. Halfway down the hill towards the town Molly braked sharply and pulled into the side of the road. Above the hill the female peregrine was circling on the warm air. Suddenly it made a fast and ferocious stoop for its prey, so that George held his breath in wonder, as if he too were diving at that speed, with the air rushing past his face. Then the bird was gone and Molly drove on. He looked at her with gratitude because she had seen the bird and had stopped for him to enjoy it too. The image of exhilaration, wildness and beauty remained with him, as an image of his home, and he knew he would return there and remember it with pleasure.

CPSIA information can be obtained
at www.ICGtesting.com
Printed in the USA
FSHW010702140221
78617FS